BY MAME FARRELL

Marrying Malcolm Murgatroyd

Bradley and the Billboard

BRADLEY AND THE BILLBOARD

MAME FARRELL

BRADLEY and the BILLBOARD

Farrar, Straus and Giroux
New York

Distributed in Canada by Douglas & McIntyre Ltd.

Printed in the United States of America

Designed by Caitlin Martin

First edition, 1998

12 11 10 9 8 7 6 5 4

Library of Congress Cataloging-in-Publication Data

Farrell, Mame.

    Bradley and the billboard / Mame Farrell. — 1st ed.

      p.   cm.

    Summary: When thirteen-year-old Brad, a baseball hero,
gets a job as a fashion model, he must come to terms with
his ideas of what it is to be a real guy.

    ISBN 0-374-30949-3

    [1. Models (Persons)—Fiction.   2. Baseball—Fiction.

3. Identity—Fiction.]   I. Title.

PZ7.F2455Br   1998

[Fic]—dc21   97-36426

To Dad, with love.

Special thanks to David Speranza,
for his helpful early read.

BRADLEY AND THE BILLBOARD

CHAPTER ONE

Play Ball!

"No batter! No batter!" called the catcher, pounding his mitt. "Put 'er here!"

Brad grinned, ignoring the chatter. He just choked up on the bat, swung it into position above his right shoulder, and dug his spikes into the dirt around home plate.

The count was 2–2. On the mound, Skeff Parker sneered. "Man, I hate pitchin' to pretty boys." He glanced over his shoulder. "You outfielders might as well take a knee."

But Brad didn't flinch.

"No batter!" the catcher repeated.

Brad recognized the first pitch, almost before it left Skeff's hand. Fastball—never one of Parker's best. This one came high and outside. *Very* high and outside. The catcher had to stretch to catch it.

"Ball!" shouted the umpire, T.J., who was Brad's neighbor. T.J. was older, but in spite of that, he was one of Brad's best friends. Their usual ump was Bernie Klemp, who was thirteen years old, like the rest of them. Bernie wasn't much of a ball player, but he had a good eye, and what T.J. called "integrity," so the guys let him umpire. Bernie was reliable, too, but today he'd had an orthodontist appointment. So T.J. was called in to sub. None of the guys minded when T.J. filled in, even if he was a friend of Brad's, because T.J. was fair to the core and everyone knew it.

Except Skeff. *"Ball?"* He slammed his glove to the ground and threw his arms up. "Oh, *man*! Get outta here!"

"Ball," said T.J. patiently.

Skeff kicked his glove. "Whadda you, *blind*? Come *on . . .*"

Brad stepped away from the plate and watched as T.J. calmly headed for the pitcher's mound. A few outfielders and the second baseman went, too. The catcher, Norman, didn't bother; he looked as disgusted as Brad. This was typical. Skeff was a jerk; even his own teammates thought so. No one in his right mind would contest that call.

"For Pete's sake," Brad grumbled to the catcher, "that pitch almost landed in the bleachers."

Norman nodded, then smiled. "Speaking of the bleachers . . . Did you see who showed up?"

Brad allowed himself a quick glance. There were rarely spectators at summer pickup games like this one. But today there was actually a turnout. A small but important turnout. There, on the bottom bleacher, right along the first-base line sat a bunch of girls, maybe six or seven. And right in the middle of the group was Jessie Brock.

Brad ground his spikes into the dust again—he had a strange feeling he might actually topple over if he didn't. Automatically, his hand went to the brim of his cap. He removed it and quickly dragged his fingers through his hair. He didn't even know he was doing it.

Norman laughed. "You gonna powder your nose, too? Jeez!" He gave Brad a friendly punch to the shoulder.

"When did she get here?" Brad tried to sound as if he didn't care at all.

"Around the third inning, I guess."

"Oh."

Perfect. That would mean she'd missed the stupid error he'd made in the second—and, other than that, he was having a good day.

The commotion at the mound had subsided, and T.J. was returning to the plate. One of the girls called, "Do it, Brad!" but it didn't sound like Jessie.

T.J. paused beside Brad and gave him a wink. "Looks like you've got a fan, Romeo."

Brad was just able to stop himself from smiling like a dope. He gripped the bat and said nothing.

T.J. took his place behind Norman, who had returned to a squat and was lowering his mask.

"Play ball!"

On the mound, Skeff quit sulking and got down to business.

"Who taught ya' that stance, Wilson? Your grandmother?" He laughed. "Was that before or after she taught you to knit?"

Brad felt his stomach churn. Skeff had no way of knowing, but there was more truth to his joking than Brad wished to consider. So he could knit—so what? He could hit, most of the time, and with T.J.'s coaching his pitching was improving daily. Knitting had nothing to do with anything . . . did it?

The churning in his stomach turned to a steady blaze of anger. He adjusted his feet at the plate and vowed never to pick up another knitting needle as long as he lived.

"Play ball," T.J. commanded again.

Skeff gave Brad a long, piercing stare. His right hand was behind his back; Brad imagined Skeff's fingers, arranging themselves on the laces. Curveball? Fastball? Sinker? All of a sudden, he couldn't make an accurate guess.

Skeff narrowed his eyes once more and went into his windup. *Left knee up, hands over head, long step forward* . . . The movement was fast and fluid. Skeff had good form, for a jerk.

. . . *Release!*

In that instant, Brad's anger ignited. Something sparked, something exploded . . . and he was about to find out just how good a day he was having.

He focused as the ball came into range, blazing toward him like a small white comet—his eyes held it. He clutched the bat and lifted his left foot, stepping into his swing, straight and hard, and bringing the bat around, smooth and level, and with every ounce of strength in his body.

He connected—and the earsplitting sound of wood against leather, the sharp, sweet *crack,* announced a good solid hit. The comet went blazing back in the direction from which it had come, only higher, and faster.

Brad dropped the bat and ran. His spikes hit first base. He heard someone shouting, "Go, Bradley," and this time he knew it was Jessie. She was so close he had to remind himself to keep running.

Brad was turning toward second when he heard another miraculous sound, a sound never before heard by thirteen-year-olds on the Haverton Middle School baseball diamond. It was the sound of a speeding baseball reaching the end of its journey against the billboard above and beyond the center-field fence. The sound came once, then again, pounding back on itself in an echo. After that—silence.

And suddenly no one was moving except Brad. He was running. He was still running, although he didn't actually have to. The ball was gone. Out of the park. And not just out of the park—302 feet—as *far* out of the park as that billboard, that huge, evasive, distant billboard.

So, technically, Brad could have stopped running. But he knew if he had, if he even so much as slowed down, if he wasn't *running,* he'd be *dancing.* Dancing in celebration, dancing for sheer joy, dancing with elation over being the first and only thirteen-year-old ever actually to slam a ball into that billboard beyond center field.

So he ran. And as his spikes hit home plate there was still no sound, just the memory of that ball against the billboard.

Then everyone moved at once. T.J. grabbed Brad in a bear hug and swung him around. The catcher was jumping up and down, screaming, "All right! You killed it, Wilson. Man, you *killed* it."

Brad's teammates were running over from the bench to congratulate him, and the guys on the other team came pouring in from the field to shake his hand.

Jessie Brock was on her feet, with the sun in her hair, and she was clapping and smiling at him.

Bernie Klemp, wearing his headgear, had just gotten out of his mother's car at the curb. He came running toward the backstop. "Whuck zappent? Whuck dith I mith?"

The substitute umpire was now hoisting the hero up and onto the shoulders of the other players. "Brad just hit the billboard!" T.J. told Bernie.

But before Bernie could offer his response, Skeff Parker sauntered in from the mound. He narrowed his eyes at Brad again, as if he were about to pitch another sinker.

"So what?" Skeff pulled off his glove. "Betcha can't do it again!" With that, the pitcher threw his glove down into the dust like a gauntlet.

The challenge was on.

Brad tossed his glove onto the front seat of T.J.'s car and climbed in after it. His mind spun like a Tilt-A-

Whirl, and he had the feeling he could actually glow in the dark if he wanted to. He'd *hit* the *billboard*! He'd *punished* the billboard! Jessie had seen it and Skeff had seen it, and Brad, of course, had seen it, which was a good thing because, if he hadn't, he'd have never believed it.

T.J. seemed to be reading his mind. "It wasn't a fluke, pal. It was a good clean crack."

Brad nodded, glancing back at the field through the haze of dust T.J.'s tires stirred up. "I always thought it would be Skeff to do it first," he said honestly.

"But he didn't," T.J. reminded him. "You did."

"Weird, huh?" Brad leaned back in the seat, feeling happy and curious. He knew he wasn't the best ball player in Haverton. Not even the second best. He did know he had great baseball genes—his father had gone to college on a baseball scholarship, so heredity was on his side. Still, it always surprised him on those occasions when genetics kicked in and turned this slightly-above-average player into an all-star. "I wonder if it was just dumb luck."

T.J. shook his head. "No," he said firmly. "No way." He flipped on his blinker and for a moment the only sound in the car was the ticking of the turn signal. "I've played ball for years, Brad, and I don't think I've ever met a kid who loves this game like you do."

Brad sighed. "Then you'd think I'd be better at it, wouldn't you?"

"It's there," said T.J. "You proved that today. And besides, I didn't see Jessie standing up to cheer for Skeff when he stole third."

"He always steals third," Brad grumbled, and T.J. grinned.

"That's the point," he said, turning into his driveway.

Brad got out of the car and thanked T.J. for the ride.

"No problem," T.J. answered. "And hey—nice goin' today. You made me proud."

Brad smiled his gratitude, then scrunched through the space in the hedge that separated his small yard from T.J.'s. He found his mother and Aunt Jill on the front porch, sipping iced tea while his seven-year-old sister, Meggie, ran back and forth through the sparkling spray of the sprinkler.

"I'm back," Brad announced to the females. He knew that in twenty seconds T.J. would be scrunching through the hedge after him.

"Hi, sweetheart." His mother reached over and poured some iced tea into a glass for him.

"Hi, Jill."

"Hi, Brad." Aunt Jill flipped a page of the magazine she was reading. She didn't even look to see if T.J. was coming, because she knew he was, just as surely as Brad did. She sat calmly, and Brad knew she was silently ticking off the countdown: *Five, four, three, two* . . .

"Uh, hi . . ." came T.J.'s voice through the break in the hedge. "Brad forgot his mitt."

"Oh," said Brad, reaching out for the glove. "Thanks."

He hadn't forgotten it, actually; he'd purposely left it on the front seat. If it wasn't for Brad planting mitts and spikes and junk for T.J. to return, the poor guy would never get up the guts to come over.

Brad's mom smiled and said hello to T.J., and Meggie came over to give him a drippy hug. Then Brad gave his friend a nudge to the ribs; T.J. cleared his throat.

Aunt Jill still hadn't bothered to look up. Brad wanted to laugh, but he actually felt for T.J. When it was a guy against a girl in this kind of game, Brad knew most guys didn't stand a chance.

T.J.'s voice was on the verge of cracking when he finally said, "Hi, Jill."

Jill looked up as if she hadn't even noticed he was there. "Oh. Hi, T.J." She went back to her magazine. Brad could tell from the look on T.J.'s face that the wheels in his brain were turning frantically, trying to come up with the right thing to say.

"Um," he began, "that's a nice shirt. Is it new?"

Jill gave a casual glance to the blouse she was wearing and shook her head. "Nope. Had it for years."

Brad shook his head. Typical rookie error—don't compliment a woman on her clothes unless you *know* what you're talking about.

T.J. tried again. "Hot out, huh?"

Jill didn't even look up.

Brad bit back a chuckle. T.J. was going down swinging. It was time to bring in a designated hitter—in this case, that would be Brad.

"So, Jill," he said carelessly, "did Chase Stanton finally propose?"

At this, T.J.'s eyes went wide, and Brad had to laugh because he knew what T.J. was thinking.

"No!" Jill's eyes were shining. "He didn't! He was going to, but, you see, what he and Bethany didn't realize was that witch Magdelena had arrived in town just that morning. She was supposedly locked up in some asylum somewhere, but, of course, she knocked out an orderly and escaped."

Brad gave T.J. a nudge, soliciting a comment, but the best T.J. could come up with was a blank-faced nod.

Jill continued gravely. "Anyway, Magdelena—who, remember, used to be married to Brooks, *before* his sex change, but *after* his amnesia—broke into Bethany's guest house and disguised herself as a nun, which was stupid, because everyone knows there's only one nun in Fort Stevens—Sister Bernard, who's now totally blind, but still acting as nurse to Gloria Wentworth-Santiago, who, of course, has been in a coma since that volcano erupted while she was in Peru . . ."

"Right," said T.J., who seemed to have finally caught on. "Since the volcano erupted . . . Peru."

"Do you watch the soaps?" Jill asked sweetly.

T.J. began to shake his head, but when Brad threw him a look, he changed his answer fast. "I mean . . . yeah. You know, once in a while . . . the hospital one, if I get home from work early."

For this, T.J. was rewarded with one of Jill's glowing

smiles. "My favorite," said Jill, and T.J. sighed thankfully, as if he'd just been saved from an untimely death. Then he remembered Brad's big news.

"Hey, guess what! Brad just cracked a homer that hit the billboard! No thirteen-year-old kid's ever hit the billboard—most of the high school guys are still trying! That ball must have gone three hundred feet."

"Three hundred and two," said Brad, his aunt, and his mother in unison. And then the screams began.

"Way to go, Slugger!" cheered Jill, offering Brad a high five. "You finally did it!"

"Ho-ly cow . . ." cried his mother, doing her best Phil Rizzuto impression.

Meggie was hollering and turning cartwheels all over the lawn, and when Nana came out to the porch and heard the news, she put two fingers into her mouth and let out a string of high-powered whistles that made T.J.'s jaw drop.

Brad removed his hands from his ears and rolled his eyes. "You think this is big, you should have seen them when I decided to add macadamia nuts to my chocolate-chip cookie recipe."

T.J.'s eyebrows shot up in surprise. "*Your* chocolate-chip cookie recipe?"

Brad immediately wished he hadn't mentioned it. Then his mother caught Brad in a hug and covered his cheeks with kisses.

"Thanks, guys," said Brad, wiggling free. He'd never seen Skeff Parker's mother cover Skeff with kisses for an out-of-the-park homer. Then again, he'd never seen Skeff Parker's mother at all.

"We should celebrate!" said Nana from the porch.

"Yes," Brad's mother agreed. "Why don't we all go out for dinner tonight! T.J., you come, too."

At this, Brad's happiness dissolved. "Uh . . . that's okay, Mom. Really. It's not that big a deal."

"Don't be ridiculous, Brad." His mother planted her hands on her hips. "It's an incredibly big deal! You've been yapping about clobbering that old billboard for ages!" She gave him a brave smile.

"Mom, really . . ." Brad swallowed hard. "We don't have to."

But Mom waved her hands and laughed again. "I wasn't talking about champagne and caviar! Come on! I think we can splurge on a few cheeseburgers and some chocolate shakes."

Aunt Jill put a hand on Brad's shoulder. "I've got some extra cash," she said, giving him her prettiest smile. "I gave a haircut to a little old lady today that made her look fifteen years younger, and she gave me a huge tip. I can't think of anything I'd rather spend it on than your victory dinner."

Brad smiled at his mother and his aunt. He wanted to say thank you, but for some reason he couldn't shake the tightness in his throat. Instead, he turned to T.J.

"You in?"

"We'd love to have you," said Nana, giving T.J. a wink

and motioning toward Jill. "Some of us more than others."

T.J.'s face went red. "I . . . uh, I really wish I could, but I've gotta work tonight."

Jill tilted her head and gave him a practiced pout. "That's too bad," she said sweetly. "We'll miss you."

Brad had never seen T.J. look so disappointed. He figured that little head-tilt number had very nearly stopped T.J. from breathing. It was actually sad. Hilarious, but sad.

Then Meggie was shouting, "Cheeseburgers! Cheeseburgers! *Cheese*burgers," and running into the house, before Mom could even say "Wipe your feet."

Brad was waiting for the women to get ready, which he knew could take decades. He didn't mind, exactly; it would give him some time alone in the basement.

He opened the door to the familiar dampness, and made his way down the wooden stairs toward the corner of the cellar where, six years ago, the day after his father was buried, he'd brought his father's scrapbooks and trophies. Later, he'd asked T.J. to help him drag Dad's favorite old recliner down there, too, and although he'd never had to make the request, from that time on, the women in the house respectfully left the place alone. This was his place; there was not an emery board or hair roller within a forty-foot radius.

Brad climbed into the chair, put his feet on the footrest, and leaned back, looking once again at the carefully arranged rows of baseball trophies and the framed photographs of his dad in his various uniforms: Little League, Babe Ruth All-Stars, High School Varsity. Light from the small window near the ceiling shone in behind the trophies and made them glow.

Then he picked up the scrapbook from its place on an old table and opened it. The musty smell of old paper made him feel safe and welcome. He turned to the back section, which had been unused until Brad had claimed it for himself. Then he slipped his old bat-shaped Yankees pen out from where he kept it, tucked into the book's binding. He shook the pen, coaxing the ink toward the tip.

He wrote the date. The scratch of the pen on the page was the only sound in the stillness of the cellar. *"Brad Wilson hits center field billboard. Fans go wild."*

He noted the final score, and in very small letters added, *"J.B. in bleachers."* Then he flipped forward a few pages to study some of his dad's old headlines. He ran his finger along the border of a photograph, and thought about what T.J. had said—it wasn't just dumb luck.

Brad frowned. Maybe it was frustration over Skeff riding him—not that that was unusual. Maybe it was fury, pure and simple. Brad had been mad at not being able to guess what pitch Skeff was going to throw; he'd been mad at being a better knitter than hitter.

A corner of a yellowed newspaper article that had come unglued fluttered when Brad sighed into the book. He knew the difference between lipstick and lip gloss, but when Skeff was on the mound, he could barely tell a slider from a curveball. Brad studied the book in his lap for a moment, rolling the pen between his fingers. So maybe that was what did it—the anger, the frustration. Maybe that was what clicked today, to knock that damn ball to hell.

"To hell!" he said out loud, and grinned. This was the only place in the house where he'd ever dare use a four-letter word—except, perhaps, in front of Nana, who, in spite of her soft voice and perfect makeup, could curse like a sailor when she felt like it.

For the most part, though, this house was the most ladylike place on earth, and it was starting to drive Brad crazy. Flowers blooming in every vase, wet bras and panty hose hanging from every towel rack. That in itself wasn't so bad—except that, somewhere along the way, and quite against his will, Brad had become an authority on all things feminine! Panty hose, for example—he was a panty-hose *expert*. At a glance, he could tell to whom a drip-drying pair belonged just by the size, the brand, the color. Mom always bought control top; Jill wore only suntan (which Brad agreed looked more natural than nude), and Nana wore the kind with "all-day support." He knew these stats as well as he knew his own batting average. He'd never cared before that he knew the difference between sheer and opaque—lately, though, it was beginning to bug him.

"Knocked it to hell," Brad repeated, closing the book carefully.

He sat quietly for a while, watching the trophies shimmer and studying the pictures.

Then Nana was calling down the stairs for him to come up and help Meggie with her hair, and the spell was broken. He could hear Aunt Jill squealing over the color of his mother's new eyeshadow.

It was girls' night out, and even though Brad wasn't one of the girls exactly, sometimes he sure as heck felt like it.

"Phew!" said Brad, leaning back in the booth and patting his belly. "I'm stuffed!"

"Me, too!" said Meggie, licking a glob of ketchup from her wrist. "That was the greatest dinner I ever had!"

Aunt Jill poked at the remains of her meal—one soggy cucumber and a smashed cherry tomato. She sighed. "The salad was a bit of a letdown."

Brad rolled his eyes. "It's a burger joint," he told her. "Look at the sign, for Pete's sake. It doesn't say 'Billions and Billions of *Salads* Sold,' does it?"

"No, it doesn't," Jill agreed. "And now I know why!"

Nana Wilson was finishing up her french fries with dainty little bites. "So tell us again, Bradley. How did it feel to hit the billboard?"

Brad closed his eyes and a slow, wide smile spread across his face. He would be happy to tell them again . . . and again . . . and again. But he'd just polished off his third large soda and at the moment he had to excuse himself.

He passed purposely close to the service counter, to see if the cute girl at the cash register would smile at him again as she had when she'd taken his burger order. Brad lingered at the straw dispenser a moment, but when he saw that the girl was too busy counting change to notice him, he went to the men's room.

Brad was washing his hands when Skeff came crashing out of a stall.

Brad eyed him in the mirror. "Well, that explains the stench in here."

"Ha, ha." Skeff gave him a dirty look. "Is your mommy gonna check to see if you scrubbed your fingernails?" he taunted.

Brad dried his hands on a paper towel. "When did you get here?" he grumbled. He was glad he hadn't seen Skeff earlier. Otherwise, he would have lost his appetite.

"Just now," said Skeff with a smirk. "I've got this scam going—I tell the guys to order for me, cuz I gotta pee. By the time I get out, they've already paid for the food, and then I just conveniently forget I owe 'em the money."

Brad ignored him and headed for the door, but Skeff stepped into his path, cutting him off.

He gave Brad a look of mock horror. "What's this? Isn't the pretty boy even gonna check his hairdo? Huh? I thought you glamorous types get nervous when one hair is out of place."

"Pretty boy?" Brad lowered his eyebrows and gave Skeff a shove that sent him smashing into the trash can. "What's your problem, Parker?"

"You are, Mr. Big. Mr. Billboard. You got lucky today."

"I'd like to see you do it, Parker," Brad growled.

"I will. Right after *you* do it again! Don't forget! Everybody heard me dare you."

Brad glared at Skeff and said nothing. He'd forgotten about that stupid challenge, but Parker was right—everyone had heard.

Skeff gave Brad an evil smile, turned, and walked out of the bathroom.

Brad's mind was racing. All he could think of was how in one afternoon that billboard had become the biggest thing in his life. When Brad reached the table, his family was ready to leave.

Distracted, he followed them to the parking lot. Climbing into the car after Meggie, he could hear all that "pretty boy" garbage ringing through his head.

But Brad forgot that when he spotted Skeff coming out of the restaurant with his buddies. He had his bag full of free food all right . . . but he also had half a roll of toilet paper stuck to his shoe. It was dragging along behind him and the kids in the parking lot were laughing.

As their car pulled past the cluster of guys, Brad rolled down his window and stuck his head out.

"Hey, Parker," he shouted. "Don't forget to pay your buddies back for that Happy Meal."

"That's right, ya' big mooch," said one of Skeff's sidekicks. "Pay up!"

Brad rolled up the window, settled back against the seat, and smiled to himself.

CHAPTER TWO

Safe at Home

Brad sat on the couch with his arms folded. A funky old disco tune blared through the room.

"Lighten up, will ya'?" cried Nana, who was shaking her hips wildly.

Brad frowned and willed his feet not to tap.

Aunt Jill, in some gooey green facial mask, was tugging at his elbow. The stuff stank of cucumber, and her hair, wound up in Velcro rollers, was damp with the fragrance of her coconut-scented styling mousse. This was his life—cucumber and coconut and Velcro rollers. He sighed heavily.

Brad was willing to bet that Skeff Parker had never been this close to a Velcro roller in his life—or if he had been, he certainly wouldn't have known what to call it. But Brad did. He also knew that Velcro rollers gave "lift" and "body" rather than curl, and the fact that he knew this made his stomach churn.

"Dance, Bradley!" Jill giggled, tugging harder.

Meggie was shaking her whole little body like someone in the throes of a convulsion. "Do the Bradley Boogie!" she pleaded. "Do the Bradley Boogie!"

Brad grinned in spite of himself. The Bradley Boogie—he'd invented it, perfected it, and on nights like this, when his mom and aunt and sister and grandmother got into one of their giddy, slumber-party moods, he'd sometimes join in with the combination disco/hip-hop/two-step dance that was his and his alone.

"I've quit dancing!" he said firmly, and added this vow to his no-knitting oath.

Mom stuck her tongue out and executed a little spin.

Nana did a Charleston number that made everyone whoop, and then Meggie tried it and landed on her rump. She recovered with a somersault and Brad found himself itching to spring up and take part in this familiar ritual.

He closed his eyes. He ground his teeth.

But the music seemed to electrify the room, until Brad could sit still no longer. The next thing they knew, he was on his feet, shaking, shimmying, and sashaying with more rhythm than the three of them put together.

"That's my boy," cried Mom.

"Wooh!" cried Nana, clapping her hands. "Go, Bradley! Go, Bradley! Go, Bradley!"

When the song ended, everyone flopped down on the sofa, exhausted.

"I think I burned off those cheeseburgers," Mom said, breathlessly.

Brad cringed. He knew what was coming next.

"Who needs a manicure?" cried Jill.

Who didn't? Mom, Nana, and Meggie raised their hands enthusiastically, and Brad, always the gentleman, went to the refrigerator to get the nail enamel. In his house, sometimes there was more nail polish in the fridge than there was food.

He returned to the family room with a handful of the small, cool bottles and handed each female her favorite. Red Alert for Nana, Peachy Keen for Mom. Aunt Jill was a big fan of Earthy Taupe (which Brad had always thought should be called Dirt), and to Meggie, who was still working on growing her nails, he held out a bottle of clear, gelatin-enriched strengthener.

"No frost?" she asked, taking the polish.

Brad shook his head. "Mom used the last of it to head off a run in her nylons."

"Hey," cried Jill, "did anyone tape *Mercy General* today? Garth was supposed to hypnotize Hillary and then run off with her stepmother!"

"The VCR's on the blink," Mom reported. "And there isn't any extra money in the kitty."

Brad wagged his eyebrows at Jill. "Maybe T.J. saw it. Why don't you give him a call and ask him what happened?"

Jill blew on the nails of her left hand, trying to hide her smile. "I would," she said, handing Brad the polish and holding the fingers of her right hand out to him. "But I'm afraid the poor thing would drop dead of a heart attack."

Brad bit his lip in concentration, carefully applying the Earthy Taupe to his aunt's pinkie. "He's shy," he said, dipping the brush back into the bottle. "He's insecure."

"T.J.'s a babe," said Meggie.

Nana laughed. "What's he got to be insecure about?"

"Nana!" said Brad.

"What? I call 'em as I see 'em, kiddo! That T.J. is a hunk. Just like you!"

"Brad's too young to be a hunk," teased Meggie. "He's still just a hunkling."

Brad rolled his eyes. He was used to hearing how cute he was. From Nana, her bridge ladies, his mother . . . Skeff calling him a pretty boy was new, though, and Jessie Brock had never showed up at the field before.

Jill was going on about her uncertain relationship with T.J. "Did you see him today? He was helpless."

"That's because you won't give him a break," snapped Brad. "Why can't you quit playing head games and tell him you like him already?"

Nana gave Brad a nudge to the ribs. "I think Jill *likes* driving T.J. nuts."

"I do," Jill confessed, grinning. "But, believe me, he'll definitely forgive and forget when we finally . . ."

Mom covered Meggie's ears fast. "Jill!"

Jill giggled, then examined Brad's handiwork on her nails. "Perfect, as always."

Brad should have been glad to hear it. But he couldn't help wondering if a guy's aunt telling him his manicure technique was "perfect as always" could be considered a form of cruel and unusual punishment.

Why couldn't someone in this house challenge him to an arm wrestle? Or a burping contest? This thought left him feeling lonely and guilty at the same time, and he wondered what Skeff Parker was doing right at that moment. Not somebody's nails, he was sure of that.

Then the conversation turned to Garth, Hillary, and her stepmother, and in spite of himself, Brad jumped in, offering his opinions on this steamy love triangle.

The next day, Brad awoke to the sound of the phone ringing. He rolled over, then flipped his pillow so that the cool side was now beneath his cheek. It was only eight-thirty and already it was sweltering.

He was just drifting back to sleep when he heard a gentle knock on his door.

"Bradley?" came Mom's voice. "Telephone."

Brad sat up, yawning. "For me?"

He got up and padded across his room and into the family room, toward the phone. He could see Nana in the kitchen, sitting at the table with a towel around her neck, while Aunt Jill put scrawny plastic rollers in her hair. Wonderful, Brad thought, reaching for the phone.

Another home permanent. The house'll stink for days. It was one more hardship that came of living with a bunch of women. At least this time he hadn't been conned into helping Jill *give* the stupid perm—a skill he'd been perfecting since he was Meggie's age.

His mother handed over the receiver with a weird silly smile on her face. She didn't seem to want to leave. She just stood there, giving him that goofy grin.

"Uh, thanks . . ." said Brad.

His mom stood grinning a second longer before she walked away. Brad figured the fumes from perm lotion were destroying her brain. But then he overheard Mom telling Nana and Jill in a whispery voice, "It's a girl!"

"Hello?"

"Bradley? Hi. It's Jessie."

His heart felt as if it were sliding into third. "Hi. Uh . . . hi. How are you?"

"Fine, thank you. How are you?"

"I'm okay." He hoped this was how a phone conversation with a girl was supposed to go. After all, he hadn't had much practice. He'd listened to Jill talk to guys on the phone thousands of times, but, of course, that had been the wrong end of the conversation. "What's going on?" he asked, and his voice only broke a little.

Suddenly Brad felt embarrassed to be standing there in just his pajama bottoms talking to Jessie Brock. Then he felt stupid for being embarrassed.

"Well," said Jessie, "I just wanted to say congratulations on your billboard shot."

Brad's hands were so sweaty he was surprised the phone didn't slip out of the hand that was holding it. "Thanks," he said, then added in a modest voice, "It was nothing."

Jessie giggled. "Three hundred and two feet is definitely not nothing."

He was about to ask how she knew the exact distance but she giggled again and it was such a sweet, incredible sound that it made him forget his question.

"My older brother's been trying to reach it for years. We've got this ongoing bet about who in our family is going to hit it first."

Brad smiled to himself. Jessie was always one of the first girls to get chosen when they played softball in gym class. He found it kind of cute that she actually believed she had a chance to slam the billboard. He didn't get to tell her so.

"So, anyway," said Jessie, "a bunch of us are going down to the lake today."

"Yeah? Cool."

"I wanted to tell you, in case . . . you know . . . in case you wanted to come, too."

"Sounds great."

He could tell from her voice that Jessie was smiling now, too. "We're all gonna meet at the picnic tables around eleven."

"Okay. I'll see ya' there."

"Okay. Bye, Brad."

"Bye, Jessie." He hung up the phone. Had that really

happened? Or was he still dreaming? He turned and headed for the kitchen, where he discovered that now all three of the women had weird silly smiles on their faces. It was real, all right. Jessie Brock had called and invited him to the lake. He wanted to shout that he was the luckiest guy in Haverton Middle School.

But all he said was, "Orange juice?"

"In the fridge," said his mother.

Brad opened the door to the refrigerator and hunted around for the juice carton. When he found it, he turned around to find a strange sort of silence had settled over the kitchen. Meggie had joined the other three females and now they were all *staring* at him with their dopey smiles.

"What?"

Aunt Jill took a deep breath and let it out in the dreamy way she sometimes did when one of her soap-opera characters reunited with an old flame or got married.

"What?"

Meggie bit into an English muffin. "We're just a little promotional, that's all."

"Promotional?"

Mom laughed softly. "She means emotional, honey."

"Emotional?" Brad looked from one woman to the next, playing dumb. "Since when does a glass of orange juice get you guys so worked up?"

Nobody answered. Brad sipped his juice warily, watching them as they watched him, still smiling those goofy smiles. "You didn't get the pulpy kind," he said to his mother.

Mom's expression didn't change. "Sorry, sport. No coupon."

He took another sip, and they went right on looking. And looking. He had taken just about all he could take when suddenly Nana Wilson began to laugh.

"Now what?" asked Brad.

"I was just thinking about the first time a girl called your father."

"A girl called Dad?" Brad glanced over at his mom, not sure this was an appropriate conversation to be having in front of her.

Nana went on, handing another curler over her shoulder to Jill. "He got all nervous and his cheeks turned pink." Now Nana was looking at Brad's mother, who, Brad noticed, was turning a little pink herself.

"I don't know where I got the guts," said Mom, spooning some sugar into her coffee.

Brad almost choked on his orange juice. "*You?* You were the first girl who ever called Dad?"

Mom nodded. "And the last." She raised one eyebrow. "As far as I know, anyway."

Nana laughed. "The first, the last, and the only, and you know it. He never even knew another girl existed once he met you!"

"I suppose now we'll have to do our moral duty," Jill said, cracking a smile, "and whip this kid into shape. Get him to his dating weight, so to speak!"

"What's that supposed to mean?" Brad demanded. "Whip me into what shape?"

"Oh, big brother of mine," teased Meggie. "There is much for you to learn!"

"Like what?" said Brad.

"Like," said Jill, "for example, when you tell a young lady you are going to *call* her, what do you do?"

"I dunno," said Brad.

"You *call* her!" cried Nana and Mom in unison.

Brad smiled. Aunt Jill was always complaining about guys who said they would call but didn't. "Okay. If I say I'll call . . . I call. What else?"

"When a girl says no, it means no," said Mom, a bit seriously. "And if you don't know what I mean right this minute, young man . . ."

Brad was no dummy—he knew what that meant. "Continue . . ."

"Don't try to bamboozle the gals," Nana warned. "Lay off the macho stuff and just be yourself."

Brad felt a stab of panic. "Are you saying I'm not macho?"

"Yes, that's exactly what I'm saying," she told him. "You're much better than macho."

"Oh." Brad would have to ponder this one; but he figured if it came from Nana it must be good advice.

"Give girls presents," said Meggie with an air of experience. "Lots of good presents. Presents are key, Brad. Presents!"

"Kiss with your eyes closed . . ."

". . . never ask her how much she weighs . . ."

". . . shake hands with her father . . ."

". . . no burping, no farting . . ."

". . . don't panic if she asks you to hold her purse . . ."

Brad drank up the advice they poured out to him. When the clock in the family room chimed ten o'clock, Brad felt *ready.*

Ready for what, he wasn't sure. But he knew he was definitely ready.

He excused himself to get dressed, and he could hear the females talking as he left.

"Here we go . . ." his mom was saying. "This is the beginning."

He didn't waste time wondering what she meant by that, though, because he had to hurry. He was meeting Jessie Brock in an hour and he didn't want to be even one half a second late.

When he emerged from his room, a beach towel draped over his shoulder, his mother had one word for him: "Meggie."

Brad cocked an eyebrow. "Little kid, big vocabulary . . . What about her?"

His mother held out a canvas bag full of sand toys. "Would you take her along?"

"Take her along?" Brad's eyebrows shot up. "To the *lake*? Where all my friends are going to be?"

"If memory serves," said his mother, "there'll be sand and water there, too."

"Your friends don't own the lake, Brad." Meggie lifted

her chin. "*My* friend Chrissy Samuels is going to be there, too."

"So now I'm Mary Poppins?" Brad took the sand toys and glared at his sister. "I suppose I'm gonna have to *watch* her? How am I supposed to talk to Jessie if I'm watching Meggie?"

"Relax, lady killer." His mother smiled. "I called Mrs. Samuels and asked her to keep an eye on Meg in the water. All you have to do is bring her there."

Brad threw his sister a grin. "Do I have to bring her back?"

"Yes."

"Alive?"

"Preferably."

Meggie gave a squawk and Brad couldn't help smiling. "Let's go!" he said.

Brad pedaled his bike at top speed the entire three miles to the lake. When he reached the top of the long, sloping entrance, he leaned forward on the handlebars and coasted down the smooth black-topped slant toward the parking lot. Meggie clung to him from her place on the seat behind him. The air rushed past, hot against his face.

At the bottom, he could see Jessie and three of her girlfriends piling out of a station wagon. *Right on time,* he thought. He veered left, past the playground, and guided his bike over the curb of the sidewalk, where he let Meggie off, then lowered his beat-up mode of transportation to the ground.

Chrissy came bounding over to Meggie. In the distance, Brad could see Mrs. Samuels setting up her beach chair.

"See ya' later, Meg."

Meggie gave Brad a wink for good luck before heading off toward the water. "Knock 'er socks off, big brother!"

He laughed.

"Hey, Wilson!"

He turned to see his friends Scott Treeler and Trevor Wells cutting through the playground.

"Heard about your billboard shot," said Trevor, offering Brad a high five. "Awesome, man!"

Brad gave him a modest shrug. He didn't want to get carried away and have people start calling him conceited. The truth was, he'd never been good at taking compliments. Even sports compliments. Maybe because he was afraid to jinx himself.

"Parker's goin' around sayin' it was just some dumb fluke," Scott informed him. "What a creep! I heard he challenged you to hit it again."

"Yeah," said Trevor. "You think you can?"

Brad removed his towel from his shoulder and stuffed it under his arm. "All I can do is try, I guess."

They followed the sidewalk around the snack-bar pavilion toward the picnic tables. On the opposite side of the pavilion, they spotted Pamela Hartley and four of her friends coming out of the girls' bathroom.

"Pamela and her rat pack," Trevor announced. "Man, she's beautiful, but I can't stand that chick."

"Pamela Heartless," said Brad. "The girl's got a serious mean streak."

"Why do girls always have to go to the bathroom together?" Scott wondered out loud.

When they reached the picnic tables, they found the boys were seated at one, and the girls, including Jessie, at another. It took a while to say hello to everyone; Brad saved Jessie for last.

"Hi," he said, crossing over from the boys' table to the girls'.

"Hi, Bradley."

He was aware of the boys watching him. Every one of them wanted to cross over to the girls' table, but they were too scared. Or shy. Or maybe just too stupid. Brad found it pretty amusing—he ate dinner every night at a "girls' table," and for him, this was a cakewalk.

He pushed himself up so that he was sitting on the edge of the table. "New bathing suit?"

Jessie nodded. Her dark hair bounced on her shoulders and she smiled. "Do you like it?"

"It's great. Blue's a good color on you."

Skeff took one step—just one—closer to the girls' table and snickered. "Maybe he wants to borrow it!"

The boys cracked up and the girls who weren't staring at Brad with dreamy eyes began to giggle.

Pamela's giggle had an evil edge. "Brad couldn't fit into *Jessie's* suit," she announced, grinning. "Not enough chest room!" With that, she stuck out her just-sprouted baby boobs and batted her eyes at Brad.

Brad ignored her and leaned back on his elbows.

"Will your dad be coming to pick you up?" he asked Jessie. "If he is, I think I'd like to shake his hand."

Jessie seemed a little confused by that, and for a moment Brad was afraid he'd said something stupid. She was smiling at him, though, and that was a good sign. Then she asked, "Did you watch the Yankees game last night?"

"Heartbreaker," said Brad, shaking his head sadly. "They couldn't hit to save their souls."

Jessie nodded. "If that second baseman would just get out of his batting slump . . . The problem is, he's just overthinking every pitch."

"Yeah." Brad grinned. It was pretty cute, the way she was trying to impress him. Of course, he wouldn't have cared if she'd blamed last night's loss on Babe Ruth for dropping the puck and blowing the final touchdown.

The sun was warm on his shoulders and Skeff for once was keeping his mouth shut. As far as Brad could tell, there was nothing that could ruin the perfection of this moment.

Except . . . Meggie!

"Brad! I need you."

When he saw Meggie approaching, he felt his stomach drop. She was holding a comb and an elastic band, and her long hair billowed freely behind her. *No,* he begged silently. *Please, Meg, no . . .*

Meggie reached the picnic table, planted herself before her brother, then flashed her most adorable smile around the group.

"She's so sweet," Jessie whispered to the girl next to her.

At this, Brad relaxed, but only slightly. "What's up?" he asked Meggie.

"Mrs. Samuels says it'll be safer for me to swim if my hair is tied back." She handed him the comb. "Will you do it?"

There was a life-threatening lump in Brad's throat when he whispered through his teeth, "Can't Mrs. Samuels do it?"

Meggie gave him her best pout. "I like the way *you* do it!"

Skeff gave a loud hoot. "She likes the way *he* does it," he mimicked in a high voice. "That figures."

Brad felt like burying himself—better yet, burying Skeff—in the sand. "C'mon, Meg . . ."

"Mom said!" she reminded him. "You've got to bring me back alive, remember?"

Jessie looked as if she found this last remark adorable, and since Brad seemed to have no choice in the matter, he snatched the comb and the elastic and told his sister to turn around. Carefully but quickly, he separated Meggie's thick blond mane into three sections. He was aware that every eye was on him as he wrapped and tucked each piece into place. In minutes, Meggie's hair was held fast in an elegant, flawless French braid.

Brad wound the hair elastic around the bottom and let

the braid drop from his hand like some poisonous serpent.

"Thanks, Brad," piped Meggie, then skipped off toward the beach.

Brad stared down at the picnic table, poised for Skeff's next insult. His heart was pounding, but he did not move so much as one muscle. Then he sensed movement to his left; Jessie was getting up from her place on the bench. That didn't surprise him—she probably wanted to get out of there before Skeff started teasing *her* for liking a guy who knew how to braid.

The next words Brad heard, though, weren't Skeff's. The next words were Jessie's and they almost sent him into a double back flip off the picnic table.

"Will you do mine?" she was asking.

It took Brad a moment to get his voice to work. "Sure," he said. "Yeah. Sure."

Jessie smiled, then turned away from him and backed into the space where Meggie had stood to have her hair done—the space between Brad's knees. Jessie was standing between Brad's knees and her head came up to just below his nose, where he could smell the clean fruity fragrance of her hair.

"I need an elastic," he said, still not believing it, and at that request, five girls practically dove into their beach bags to find one. Melissa Abernathy found one first, and when she placed the little rubber band in Brad's palm, he could have sworn she let her fingers linger there against his hand.

He was also aware of the boys gaping from their table in stunned silence. Skeff looked furious, but the rest of them looked just plain envious.

Brad wondered how he looked. Probably elated. Or maybe terrified.

He reached out and took hold of Jessie's shining dark hair, combing it through with his fingers. He had never felt anything so luxurious in his life. It was silky smooth, and warm from the sunshine. For a moment, he didn't think he'd ever be able to let go. Slowly, he split her hair into three even sections and arranged them between his fingers. He saw her shoulders relax and thought he felt her lean her head back ever so slightly, as if the whole thing felt as wonderful to her as it did to him.

Wonderful . . .

He started braiding, guiding Jessie's hair, twisting it gently, pulling up more from the sides as he progressed. Once, his hand brushed the back of her neck, and they both jumped slightly at the surprise of it. Her skin was the softest thing he could imagine. After a moment's hesitation, she lifted her arms and rested them on his legs.

"I'm almost finished," he said.

"Take your time," she whispered, and there was a blush in her voice.

Brad had never felt so connected to anyone before— his legs, her arms, his hands, her hair . . . He continued, folding the long lengths over and over on themselves, enjoying the feeling of each and every strand against his hands, until the braid was completed. Putting in the elastic, he found himself fighting the urge to shake the braid free and start again . . . and again . . .

Instead, he let it slip from his fingers, so its brushy tip landed softly between Jessie's shoulder blades. She didn't step away, not immediately.

When she did, she thanked him with a smile.

Brad had to remind himself to breathe.

Then somebody shouted, "Race to the raft! Raft race!"

And suddenly towels were flying, shirts and shorts were being flung and sneakers were getting kicked in all directions. Everyone took off at lightning speed across the picnic area toward the sand, then down the beach to the water. At the shoreline, the girls started shrieking but the boys dove headlong into the cool blue lake, where they broke into fast, furious freestyle strokes toward the raft. The girls caught up soon enough, and then everyone was climbing the ladders and tugging friends up and out of the water, then pushing them in again.

Brad saw Jessie break the surface at the far corner of the raft and tried to look very casual as he made his way to where she was. He leaned down and offered her his hand, which she took, smiling. He held her arm securely, but not tight enough to hurt, and pulled her up onto the warm wooden surface of the float.

She sat down, and he sat down next to her. Then Pamela Hartley rushed over and gave Jessie what was supposed to be a friendly push into the water.

"Hi, Brad."

Brad grumbled, "Hi, Pam." He kept his eyes on the

water, but this time Jessie swam to the ladder and climbed up on her own.

Pamela sat down where Jessie had been sitting and gave him one of her dumb, obnoxious pouts. "You didn't say you liked *my* suit."

That's cause I don't, Brad thought. When he didn't respond, Pamela slid over so that her wet leg was pressed against his. "Brad, will you buy me a soda later?"

Brad pulled his knees up and rested his chin on them. "I can't. I forgot to bring money."

"Then *I'll* buy *you* a soda," Pamela bubbled.

"No thanks," he answered dryly.

That was when Trevor Wells skidded over and pushed Pamela, screaming, into the drink. Trevor Wells was a true friend.

After a while, everyone swam back in to the beach and sat around talking about which teachers they hoped they wouldn't get in September. Somebody started in with a great story about somebody else's older brother who got caught parking with somebody else's older sister, and everyone laughed and asked for the details, but the details never actually got told, which was fine, because nobody really wanted to hear them, anyway.

The sun rose hotter and Brad wished he had money to buy Jessie a 7-Up. One of the girls had brought along a cooler full of bottled drinks which she offered to everyone. Jessie seemed to be having a difficult time twisting off the twist-off cap on hers, so Brad opened it for her, which was almost as good as buying her a soda.

After that, the girls worked on their tans and the boys tried not to look as if they were watching the girls work on their tans. At one point, a bunch of girls from the parochial school walked by—then they walked by again, more slowly, and Brad had the very strange feeling that they were looking at him. One good glare from Pamela Hartley scared the parochial-school girls away for good, though.

At four o'clock, everyone started gathering up their belongings and heading for the parking lot to meet their rides. Brad said goodbye to Jessie and she gave him a really terrific smile and thanked him again for the braid.

Brad was walking with Trevor and Scott toward the playground when it started.

It began with some whispering, then it turned into giggles. The next thing Brad knew, Pamela and her flunkies had practically surrounded him. They were staring at him and for one insane moment Brad thought they looked a little dangerous.

He turned up his palms impatiently. "What now?"

"I just want to tell you something," said Pamela.

"So tell me."

"I want to tell you"—she began softly, then raised her voice to a full-fledged holler—"that you are a total babe!"

Brad felt his face get hot.

Pamela's friends were giggling again. "You're the cutest boy in school!" said one.

"Super *hunk*!" said another.

"Cut it out!" Brad demanded. His cheeks were burning now.

"Bradley is a total babe," Pamela announced loudly, then cupped her hands to her mouth and really screamed. *"Bradley's babelicious!"*

"C'mon, Pam," Brad pleaded, softening his tone from demanding to desperate. "Shut up, will ya'?"

Pam cocked her head at him. "Oh, don't be so modest, Brad. Why don't you just accept it? You're the hottest guy in the whole school."

Pam's friends burst into giggles of agreement. Brad looked to Scott and Trevor for assistance, but they just exchanged glances and began walking more quickly.

"Pam, just drop it," said Brad. "I'm not the—" He couldn't even bring himself to say it.

"Well, if you're not," teased Pam, folding her arms and waggling her eyebrows at him, "then who is?"

"How the heck should I know?"

"Well, then," said one of Pam's cronies, "if you don't know who the hottest boy *is,* then how do you know you're not him?"

As much as Brad hated to admit it, there was some logic to that. At the moment, though, he didn't feel like discussing it. At the moment, he felt like getting his sister, jumping on his bike, and pedaling out of there as fast as he possibly could.

Which is exactly what he did.

CHAPTER THREE

Here's the Windup . . . and the Pitch . . .

At home, Brad and Meggie found their mother just getting into the car.

"Hop in," Mom commanded.

"Where we going?"

"Shopping!"

Brad leaned his bike against the hedge and hopped into the car. He rolled down the rear window and let the wind whip his sweaty face. He probably should have gone inside to wash it first, since he knew the sand and perspiration might cause his skin to sprout a few big, ugly zits. That would put an end to his "hottest guy" status for sure. He closed his eyes tight, willing the pimples to erupt.

Mom was explaining, "Baker's is having a one-day sale."

"That's a sale," Meggie clarified, "that only lasts one day."

Brad didn't open his eyes. "Duuhhh!"

"Be nice, Bradley." Mom shot him a look in the rearview, then did a double take. "You're a mess!"

"I know." Brad stretched open the neck of his T-shirt, stuck his nose in, and sniffed. "I'm lake dirty. Sandy, sweaty, suntan lotiony."

Meggie was rolling down her window. "You stink!"

Brad gave her a broad smile. "Thanks for noticing!"

Mom turned into Baker's parking lot and scowled into the rearview. "I hate to think of you trying on new clothes in that condition."

"So I won't, then."

"We'll see about that."

Inside, their first stop was the Girls Department. Meggie made a big fuss about having to look at the 7–14 sizes. "Promotionally," she insisted, "I'm ready for Pre-Teen."

"Please," said Mom, rubbing her forehead. "Don't rush it." She and Meggie headed for the size eights.

Brad told his mother he was going upstairs to hang around the TV and stereo department.

"I'll meet you in Young Men's in half an hour," his mother called after him. "Young man."

Brad took the escalator to the second floor, where he passed through the fine china, bedding, and lingerie departments. He tried to pass through the lingerie department *fast*. Just when he thought he'd never escape the Silk and Satin Jungle, he heard the heartwarming masculine sound of electronics. He followed the sound until he came upon an entire wall of televisions, all of which were broadcasting the same program. It was truly a miracle of modern technology—fifty-some-odd TVs and every one of them tuned to Yankee baseball!

Brad meandered through the displays of VCRs, CD players, and car stereos. He passed the cellular phones and turned the corner into the camcorders section, heading for the televisions.

Then suddenly the game was gone, and in its place, in color, on fifty or so different TV screens ranging in size from portable to big-screen, was Brad Wilson's very own face.

"What the . . . ?"

He was everywhere!

Then someone was laughing. "Pretty impressive, isn't it?"

Brad turned to the camcorder counter, where a salesman was fiddling with a handheld camera, aiming it directly at Brad.

"Hold on, just . . . one . . . minute . . ." the salesman was saying, attempting to set the camera into a tripod on the countertop. He momentarily fumbled and suddenly Brad's face went haywire on fifty-some-odd TV screens.

It made Brad seasick.

"Ooops!" The salesman laughed again. "Okay. Got it . . . got it!" He secured the camera on the stand.

Brad's face was steady again.

"What do you think?" asked the salesman. "Great,

isn't it? We always have one of these set up in here. People love to see themselves on television!" He took a look at the fifty Brad Wilsons on the TV wall.

"How do I get off of there?"

"Oh, well, just step out of range, that's all. Just step to your left. There, see." He laughed. "Zap. Your TV career is over, just like that." This salesman really found himself hilarious.

Brad looked at the wall of TVs. His face had vanished; the camera was now recording the display of telephone-answering machines that had been behind him.

"Pretty impressive, isn't it?" the salesman said again.

"Yeah, sure." Brad moved on to the clock radios for a while. He waited. When the salesman was busy with a customer over in microwaves, Brad went back to where the camcorder was nestled on its tripod. He stepped in front of it.

Again, his face appeared on the screens. He smiled—all fifty of him smiled.

Brad looked around to see if anyone was watching. No one was. He leaned toward the camera (the fifty screens were now broadcasting a very tight shot of his nostrils). He hit the zoom button, then stepped back again.

Fifty extreme close-ups of Bradley Wilson pulsed through the Home Entertainment and Electronics Department.

The salesman returned then. He asked if Brad would be needing any assistance, or if he was just looking.

Brad studied his face on the screens another moment

and sighed. "Just looking, sir," he answered solemnly. "Just . . . looking."

Brad found his mother examining shirts in the Young Men's Department. She held one up for him to see.

"What do you think of this?"

"Not much."

Mom put the shirt back and held up another.

"Better."

She handed it to him, then she started in on pants. Ten minutes later, Brad was heading for the fitting room with a pile of clothes.

"Try not to sweat on them," his mother said. Then she dragged her hand through his hair a few times, combing out some sand.

Mom and Meggie waited while Brad went into the fitting room. It was empty, so he had his choice of booths. He would have expected a bigger crowd for a one-day sale. Apparently, not everyone was fortunate enough to have Meggie around to explain the concept.

He tried on the shirts first. Not bad, if he rolled the sleeves up just the right way and made his mom promise not to iron them too conscientiously. He knew that the best way to look good was to look like you weren't trying to look good.

"How you doin'?" his mother called from outside.

"Shirts fit."

He peeled off the last shirt, then dropped his shorts. They were the shorts he'd been swimming in at the lake. A small avalanche of sand spilled out of them.

Trying on the first pair of pants, Brad was vaguely aware of a voice just outside the entrance to the fitting room. It belonged to a woman who sounded very excited about something.

Brad had just stepped out of the pants when he heard the excited voice say something about TV screens and good bone structure, and then, before he knew what was happening, the door to his dressing room was flung open and there was his mother, with some lady in a business suit, standing there looking at him.

In his *underwear*!

"Hey!" He dove for his shorts.

"Oh, my!" said the lady, turning to Brad's mother. "I knew it. He's just what we're looking for."

Mrs. Wilson was beaming and looking at Brad so proudly that she didn't even seem to notice he was only wearing *underwear*.

"Really," the lady continued. "He is just so cute!"

Brad wanted to slug her. "Excuse me . . . I was changing."

The lady laughed. "Oh, you mustn't feel uncomfortable, young man. Honestly, I see people in their underwear all the time."

What kind of a sicko was she, anyway?

"You see, I *work* for Baker's. I'm in public relations."

Meggie had joined them in the fitting room now. She gave the lady a curious look. "Public relations means you see people in their underwear?"

"In a manner of speaking," the lady twittered, "yes."

By now, Brad had wriggled back into his shorts and was pulling his shirt over his head.

"Remind me not to come to any more one-day sales, will ya'?" he snapped, and stomped back toward the sales floor of the Young Men's Department.

"Brad . . ." his mother called. "Wait. Listen."

Brad stopped. He was still furious and humiliated—but where else did he have to go? The public-relations lady sashayed over.

"You see, Brad, I handle much of Baker's local advertising. I'm sure you've seen our various flyers, sale circulars, newspaper ads."

Brad shrugged. He'd seen them, all right. A bunch of dorks wearing perfectly matched, perfectly pressed clothes he wouldn't be caught dead in. He really didn't want to be standing here talking to some weird lady who'd just seen him in his underwear. "What's that got to do with me?"

"Everything, Brad. You see, you . . . *you* . . . have got the Look!"

He crunched his eyebrows down low. "What look?" If she meant the look of someone who was furious and humiliated, then yes, he probably did have it. "What are you talking about?"

"You've got the look of a model, Brad!"

Brad felt as if he'd been punched. "Model? You want me to be a model?"

"Yes!" cried the public-relations lady. "Yes, yes! I happened to be passing through Home Entertainment earlier and I saw your face on the televisions. I said to myself, now if *he* doesn't have the Look, *no one* does. Why, just look at those eyes! That hair."

Brad's mother took hold of his hair again and shook out more sand. "He's filthy," she said, apologetically. "Normally, he's a lot cleaner than this."

"Mom!"

"Well, honey . . . you *are*. Ordinarily, you're much cleaner. Isn't he, Meggie?"

Meggie held her nose. "He stinks."

"That's right," said Brad. "I stink. And I think I'm gonna be getting a whole bunch of zits, too. Any minute now, they'll be popping out all over my face. So forget it. I'm no model."

"You've got the Look," the lady reminded him.

"I'm a baseball player!"

"Variety is the spice of life," said the lady.

She *was* nuts. Brad shook his head and even more sand shot out (his mother looked as if she wanted to hide). "Can we go home now?"

"May I make a suggestion?" said the lady. "Let's go to my office and I'll explain this all to you, Brad. Maybe if I were to tell you a little about the shoot, about the job and the salary . . ."

Brad looked at his mother. "Salary? You mean . . . I'd get . . . paid?"

The lady smiled. "Let's go back to my office and talk about it, shall we?"

"Shall we?" said Meggie, being fresh.

But Mrs. Wilson didn't seem to notice that, either. She'd turned to Brad, and her expression said that the decision was entirely up to him.

Brad reached out and tugged the sleeve of a sports jacket. Then he ran his hand through a row of clip-on neckties. Then he unsnapped a jean jacket on a mannequin.

Then he said, "All right. Let's talk about it."

The lady had already seen him in his underwear—it couldn't possibly get any worse than that.

The public-relations lady's name was Ms. Heinz, and her office was on the third floor of Baker's department store, near where you had to bring your purchases if you wanted to have them gift wrapped.

Ms. Heinz sat down at her cluttered desk and smiled at Brad's mother. "You have beautiful children, Mrs. Wilson," she said. "Really. Just beautiful."

"Thank you."

Ms. Heinz gave Meggie a googly smile. "Maybe you'd like to be a model someday, too," she sang. "Just like your big brother."

"I didn't agree to be a model yet," said Brad. He wanted everyone to be clear on that.

Meggie shook her head. "No thanks. I'd rather be appreciated for my mind."

Ms. Heinz was momentarily stunned. Brad bit back a smile, and then Ms. Heinz was clearing her throat and getting down to business.

"We're doing a shoot Saturday. It's a rush-rush thing, because we'd like to start promoting our annual back-to-school bargains, ASAP."

Brad was confused. "What's an Essay Pea?"

Ms. Heinz laughed. It came out sounding rusty, as if she were out of practice, as if she didn't use laughter often. "ASAP," she repeated. "As soon as possible. We'll be doing a big push in young men's casual, which is where you come in, Brad." She leaned back in her desk chair and opened her arms. "I'm thinking youthful, boyish, but elegant, refined. Neat hair, clean fingernails, perfect creases! Class, class, class!" She punctuated each "class" with a little punch at the air.

Brad wondered how she could even use the words "boyish" and "elegant" in the same sentence.

"As I said earlier, Brad, you definitely have that Look. The Look that sells." She turned her eyes to Mrs. Wilson. "Are you interested?"

Mrs. Wilson shrugged. "It really is up to Brad. To be honest with you, I'm not sure if modeling is exactly at the top of his list of interests."

"Oh, I understand," cried Ms. Heinz, and threw up her hands as if someone were holding her at gunpoint. "I do. Believe me. I understand. Boys his age think modeling is for sissies, right? For wimps and sissies!"

Darn right, Brad wanted to tell her. He knew for a fact that, socially, neat hair and clean fingernails could actually ruin a kid.

Then Ms. Heinz was writing something on a notepad.

"There's nothing wimpy about bringing home a pay-check, though, is there, Brad?" She slid the pad across the desk to Bradley. "This is what the job pays. What do you think?"

Brad looked at the number she'd written down and his eyes went round. "Is this in dollars?" He handed the pad to his mother; her eyes went round, too.

"Of course." Ms. Heinz used her rusty laugh again. "But that's only the beginning. That number represents your hourly wage. That's how much we'll pay you per *hour.* And believe me, a big shoot like this one can last all day. It might take five, six, even seven hours to get all the material we need." She leaned back again.

Brad did the math in his head. He had never done multiplication so quickly and accurately in his life. When he came up with the answer, his heart thumped in his chest.

"You're going to give me that much money just to have my picture taken?"

Ms. Heinz smiled at him. "We at Baker's take great pride in our promotional efforts."

"We're very flattered," said Brad's mother, placing the notepad back on the desk. "I think Brad would like to have some time to think about this."

Ms. Heinz rolled a pencil between her palms and nod-ded. "Of course. Sleep on it. But I will need an answer to-morrow afternoon. As I said, the shoot is on Saturday, and if Brad is unavailable, I'll have to line up another model."

Brad cringed; he still wasn't crazy about that word. He stood up and followed his mother and Meggie to the door.

"Thank you," said Mrs. Wilson.

"My pleasure."

At the door, Brad hesitated. Then he turned, went back to Ms. Heinz's desk, and tore the sheet with his hourly wage written on it from the top of the pad. He looked at the number once more, stuffed the piece of paper in his pocket, and hurried out of the office.

He found his mother and Meggie at the elevators.

"You should do it," said Meggie decisively, then grinned. "Why waste the Look?"

"Maybe Meggie's been using the right word all along." Mrs. Wilson laughed. "Maybe you're going to be 'promotional'—*literally*—after all!"

But Brad didn't even crack a smile. He put his hand in his pocket, wrapped his fingers around the scrap of notepaper, and didn't say a word.

He wasn't sure how long he'd been sitting in the old recliner when he heard a knock on the outdoor hatchway. He stood up and crossed the basement toward the cement stairs that led outside. He unlocked the hatch and gave a firm upward shove. The rusted hinges creaked.

"I thought I'd find you here," came a voice down the short flight. Then T.J. appeared—sneakers, knees, waist, torso—ducking to clear the beams. "I tried the front door. Jill told me to check the ball field. She thought you'd be there practicing that billboard-bashing homer of yours, but . . ." He sat down on an old sawhorse and gave Brad a smile that said, *I knew better.* "I thought we were gonna watch the Yankees game together."

Brad shrugged. "Forgot."

"Brad Wilson forgot a Yankees game?" T.J. cocked an eyebrow. "Something you wanna talk about, pal?"

"I was just wondering about models."

"Planes or automobiles?"

Brad slumped into the recliner and sighed. "Humans."

T.J. cleared his throat and suddenly looked a little nervous. "Human models. You mean like the beautiful girls in evening gowns and bathing suits?"

"No. Not them. I mean, like, *guy* models. Like *kid* guy models."

T.J. didn't seem to follow. "I'm not sure I know what a kid guy model is," he confessed.

"It's *me,*" Brad groaned. "*I'm* what a kid guy model is."

"You're going to be a model?"

"Maybe," Brad muttered. "Possibly. I don't know, nothin's definite yet." Absently, his hand went to the cover of the scrapbook, lingered there a moment, then moved back to the armrest.

"How did this happen to come about?" asked T.J. "Last I heard, your only career goal was to play pro ball."

"It was. It *is.*" Brad shrugged again. "But I got discovered."

"Discovered?"

"Yeah. You probably never noticed before, but I've got the Look."

"Ah. The Look."

"Baker's department store is doing a big push in young men's casual," Brad explained.

"A big push in young men's casual, huh?" T.J. grinned.

"And they can't do a big push without the Look." Brad thumped the armrest with his palm. "Skeff Parker's been callin' me a pretty boy and this afternoon at the lake Pamela Heartless Hartley said in front of everybody that I was babelicious."

T.J. winced as if the mere thought of it was painful. Brad didn't notice there was a hint of a smile beneath it. "In front of everybody, huh?"

"Why dya' think we call her Heartless?"

T.J. got off the sawhorse and picked up a box of snapshots from where it sat atop an old dusty bureau. He looked at a few, taking more time with the pictures of Aunt Jill in her high school cheerleading uniform and prom dress. "Ya' know," he said after a while, "it's not like you've never heard it before."

"I've heard it from *bridge ladies* before," Brad clarified. " 'Brad's a cutie.' 'Oh, what a little doll.' " He sighed. "I've never heard it from a girl before!" His mouth wrinkled up into a snarl of disgust. "Or from Skeff."

"So you were hoping maybe the non-bridge ladies

of the world weren't going to catch on?" asked T.J. "You thought the girls in your grade weren't going to notice that mug of yours?"

"They don't miss a trick," Brad admitted, dragging his hands through his hair.

T.J. laughed.

"If I become a model," Brad began hesitantly, "will that mean I'm a wuss?"

"If you become a model," T.J. answered, putting the snapshots down, "I think all it'll mean is that you're a model." He leaned against the sawhorse and folded his arms. "What the heck do you care what Skeff Parker thinks? The guy's a jerk."

Brad considered this a moment. "Still . . . I keep trying to imagine what *I'd* be saying if Skeff or one of the other guys ever became a model." He was being as honest as he could be. "I'd probably give 'em a pretty hard time about it."

"Guys give guys a hard time about everything," said T.J. in his most experienced tone. "That's what guys do. Just wait till you get a girlfriend. You'll never hear the end of *that!*"

Brad climbed out of the recliner and stepped around a box of old romance novels to join T.J. against the sawhorse. "I don't give you a hard time about my Aunt Jill."

"That's because she's not my girlfriend."

Brad gave him a friendly elbow to the ribs. "Whose fault is that?"

"Hey . . ." T.J. returned the jab. "I thought we were talking about you."

"Yeah. Me." Glumly, Brad looked around the basement and considered its contents: a broken sewing machine, some old wigs on Styrofoam heads, three outdated, pore-magnifying makeup mirrors, and a collection of Jill's "I'll-never-wear-this-again" bridesmaids' gowns. He let out a long rush of breath that sent his bangs fluttering.

"It's kinda rough growin' up surrounded by girls, ya' know? Mom, Nana, Jill. Lately, even Meggie's been acting like a real girl. There's never any guy stuff goin' on in the house. No all-night poker games, no arm wrestling . . . no beef jerky."

T.J. smiled.

"And I betcha we wouldn't subscribe to any cable sports channels, even if we *could* afford 'em. But so far . . ." Brad pushed himself up so that he was sitting on the sawhorse. "So far, I think I've been holding my own. I think I've done okay. I mean, I've got an all-right batting average, and I can burp the whole alphabet."

"Yeah," said T.J. "And on top of that, you know more about the opposite sex than any guy I've ever met." He gave Brad a look to let him know how valuable such inside information was.

"I'm not a wimp," Brad went on, "or a glamour boy—at least, I don't *think* I am. And let's face it, T.J., in this house, the chances of me turning out to be a big sissy were really kinda good."

T.J. laughed gently. "Well, I grew up with three brothers, but the closest thing to an all-night poker game was playing Go Fish before bedtime. My parents sort of frowned on arm wrestling, and as far as beef jerky goes, I can't remember one stick of it ever finding its way through our front door." He put a hand on Brad's shoulder and smiled. "But I do think I know what you mean."

"If I say yes to this modeling job, if I let Baker's take my picture wearin' their dorky back-to-school clothes and let 'em put it in the newspaper or wherever, I'll be bringing home a paycheck. I can help my mom pay for stuff. For the first time, I can really be the man of the house."

T.J. nodded and crossed the basement to look at the trophies.

"It just doesn't make sense that, to be a man, I'm gonna have to do the sissiest thing in the world." Brad groaned. "I just don't know if it's possible to be a real committed athlete *and* a model."

"Sure it is," said T.J. "You ever hear of a guy named Joe Namath?"

"Broadway Joe? What about him?"

T.J. nodded. "He modeled."

"Get outta here!"

"I'm serious," said T.J. "He did this great shaving-cream commercial. And once he modeled panty hose."

"Panty hose?" Brad made a face. "Oh, man. *Panty hose?!*"

"Yeah." T.J. grinned. "It was just a big goof for the

commercial, though. And Jim Palmer—used to pitch for the Orioles—guess what he modeled."

Brad closed his eyes, afraid to even imagine. "Don't tell me it was bras, or something like that."

"Close. He modeled underwear."

"Men's underwear, I hope."

"Yes." T.J. laughed. "Men's underwear."

Brad let out a sigh of relief.

"There was even a hockey player who modeled jeans once. Ron Duguy; he played for the New York Rangers. And think of all the jocks you see doing TV commercials these days."

Brad looked skeptical. "They do sneaker endorsements and soda ads. That's not the same as modeling, is it?"

"Sure it is."

Brad allowed a moment for this information to sink in. "What if all my friends think I'm conceited? If I model, I bet they'll all think I'm stuck-up and conceited."

T.J. looked puzzled. "Why would they think you're conceited?"

"Getting my picture taken for money? You don't think that makes a guy seem conceited?"

"Let me ask you something," said T.J., picking up Brad's father's scrapbook. "Let's say, one of these days, your potential kicks in for real and suddenly you're pitchin' curves like your old man used to. Let's say your potential becomes bona-fide talent."

Brad nodded hard. That would be a dream come true.

"Okay, so now you're playing Triple A ball some-where, and a scout sees you and offers you a couple million bucks to sign with the Yanks and *use* that talent, that gift. Are you gonna take it?"

Brad's eyes widened. "Darn right I am!"

"Well, kid, that face is a kind of gift, too. Now, one of these days, the Almighty's gonna give you a killer curveball—I know it. But for the moment He gave you the Look. If you respect it, like you'd respect that curve, and use it wisely, I don't see why anybody would call you conceited." T.J. put the scrapbook down. "Besides, maybe your friends won't even see the pictures . . . unless they happen to be big fans of Baker's sales circulars."

"You know something?" said Brad, springing forward off the sawhorse. "You're right. What are the chances of anyone I know seeing one stupid little picture of me in a sales flyer?"

He allowed himself a quick look in one of the old mirrors. For the first time since Ms. Heinz had seen him in his underwear, he was beginning to think maybe being discovered wasn't going to be such a bad thing, after all.

On Friday afternoon, Brad and his mother met Ms. Heinz in her office to sign contracts and release forms. The shoot would take place the next day at one o'clock.

"Remember," Ms. Heinz told Brad, "it is very unprofessional to be late for a shoot!"

Wonderful, Brad thought miserably. Now I'm a professional pretty boy!

When Brad got home, Meggie was just hanging up the telephone. "That was Trevor," she said, handing him a piece of notepaper with the message she'd just scribbled.

"Thanks, Meg." Brad read the note once—twice, to be sure he hadn't misread it—and his stomach tightened into a knot. A ball game—a *grudge* match—was getting kicked up for Saturday morning at ten. Brad's team against Skeff's team. Actually, it was really going to be more like Brad against Skeff, and everyone, especially Brad, knew it.

"Talk about your bad scheduling!" said Meggie. Her eyes were sympathetic, but Brad didn't notice. He was staring at the note, trying to figure the time calculations. *One o'clock minus ten o'clock, factoring in nine innings . . .*

If the game went smoothly (in other words, if Skeff didn't waste a million years arguing over every call), it would probably be over by twelve o'clock. So he'd have plenty of time to get out of there and get to the shoot . . . *if* the game went smoothly.

"What if the game goes long?" asked Meggie.

"Good question." Brad bit his lower lip and thought hard. "Did Trev happen to say who was pitching?"

"Nicky Gambini," Meg answered. "You'll be his relief."

At this, the knot in Brad's stomach loosened. "Nicky's got an arm of steel. I don't think I ever saw the guy come out of a game."

"So he probably won't need you?"

Brad nodded.

"Boy, that's a"—Meggie smiled—"*relief*!"

Brad grimaced. He'd always felt it was desertion to leave a game before it was over. Even if his team was losing by a hundred, Brad believed the right thing to do was stick around and shake hands with the opponents. He may not have been the most important guy on the team, but that was no excuse for poor sportsmanship.

And if he had to leave early tomorrow, the cold hard truth was that, with Nicky on the mound, Brad's early departure would be of little or no consequence to his team; no one would even miss him. This was comforting, in a miserable sort of way.

"No problem," Brad said, more to himself than to Meggie, and tossed the note into the wastebasket. Silently, he sent up a prayer that Gambini's arm would hold up for nine innings.

Brad found his mother at the kitchen table. She was busy paying bills and didn't notice him right away. He stood quietly in the door a moment. Mom was bent over her checkbook and a piece of paper he recognized as the monthly bank statement.

He could tell, from the deep creases in her forehead and from the way she nervously punched at the calculator keys, that it was going to be difficult this month—again. He waited until she folded up the statement before he said anything.

"Hey, Mom." She looked up and Brad thought she looked very tired.

"Hi, honey." She gave him a brave smile, slid the calculator aside, and began searching the newspaper for coupons.

She cut one out and held it up for him to see. It was for fifty cents off his favorite orange juice—the pulpy kind. He wondered if "fifty cents off" meant as much in other kids' houses as it did in his. When he saw how eagerly she clipped out a dollar-off coupon for tuna fish, Brad knew that deciding to model was the right decision. He felt a little selfish for having even *considered* not doing it. He sat down heavily.

Mom tilted her head. "Got a lot on your mind?"

Brad should have been asking *her* that. He shrugged. "I just keep thinking about this modeling thing." He reached for the stack of bills beside the checkbook and absently flipped through them.

"Careful, honey. Those are in order."

Brad looked at one more closely. Phone bill. The one beneath it was for car insurance. "What kind of order do you put bills in?" he wondered.

"Well," said Mom. "The ones on top we can afford to pay, and the ones on the bottom, we can't." She attempted a chuckle, but Brad knew it wasn't funny.

"What happens when you can't pay a bill?" Brad asked softly.

"It depends." Mom held out her hand and Brad handed over the bills. Placing them in her palm gave him a strange guilty feeling, as if he'd just given her the chicken pox or a sucker punch.

"Depends on what?"

"On who we're not paying." Mom shuffled the envelopes and held one up. "The electric company, for example—they give you a grace period. That means, even if you don't pay on time, they don't just automatically shut off your electricity."

Brad glanced up at the kitchen light fixture.

Mom laughed. "Nothing to panic about, chum. We're all paid up with the electric company." She put down the bill and picked up another envelope. "Telephone," she said. "Same thing. If you don't pay one month, they just add it on to your next month's bill. They don't come by and yank your phone out of the wall immediately."

Brad remembered his call from Jessie and found himself feeling very grateful toward the telephone company. He watched his mother write out a check and slip it into the envelope.

"Doing this shoot will really help, won't it, Mom?"

She looked at him closely. "It won't hurt. But if you're having second thoughts . . ."

Brad shook his head. "It's the least I can do, don't you think? I am the man of the house."

"Yes," said Mom, as though trying not to smile.

"I don't want to keep any of the money for myself," he added. "It's all gonna go straight into the emergency puppy . . ."

"That's kitty," Mom corrected, grinning. "And that's

very generous of you, Mr. Money Bags. But really, Brad, I don't want you to go through with this modeling job if it makes you uncomfortable. My job at the pharmacy isn't bad. It gets us good health benefits, which is very important. And Aunt Jill is doing well at the salon. She helps out a lot. And Nana gets her social security check every month, and—"

"—and all of that," Brad interrupted, "all of that added together still wouldn't be as much as I'll get for just standing around having my picture taken for five hours." He looked his mother in the eye. "Would it?"

Mom reached over and took his hand. "You don't have to do it, honey. We'll be fine. We always are."

"But we could be better, couldn't we? And it's not like someone's asking me to go work in some factory or in the coal mines!" He picked up a bill and slapped it back down on the table. "All I have to do is smile and say cheese!"

"It does sound pretty crazy, doesn't it?" Mom squeezed his hand, then grinned. "Ms. Heinz was certainly pleased."

"Ms. Heinz. The Look lady!" Brad held his head. "Meggie's real cute. Why didn't Ms. Heinz discover her?"

"I suppose because Baker's isn't planning a big push in girls 7 to 14."

Brad licked a stamp and stuck it carefully on the phone-bill envelope. "It would be easier for Meggie. Nobody would think she was a sissy for being a model."

"That's true." Mom sealed the last envelope. "But she

plays soccer, and nobody thinks she's a tomboy. They just think she's a kid who plays soccer."

"It's different."

"Is it?"

He knew better than to argue the equal-rights issue in this house, so he just smiled. "I guess not," he said.

Nana appeared in the doorway then and let out a long, low wolf whistle.

"Hey, good-lookin'," she teased.

"Cut it out," said Brad, laughing.

Nana was dropping a bunch of newspaper flyers and mail-order catalogues on the table.

"What's this?"

She pulled a color circular from the stack. "Research!"

Nana handed the first circular to Brad's mother and placed another one in front of Brad.

"Research?" He frowned into the flyer. "You mean like studying?"

"Yes, like studying."

The spine of one particular catalogue in the middle of the pile caught Brad's eye and he reached for it. "I'll study this one!" he said, opening a lingerie catalogue called *Ursula's Unmentionables*.

"Nice try," said Mom, snatching it back.

Nana was muttering, "How'd that get in there?" but her eyes twinkled and she seemed to be trying not to laugh.

Brad picked up the circular Nana had given him, flipped to the boys' clothing section, and instantly knew what she'd meant by "research." The kids in the ads looked like a bunch of goofballs.

"What a waste of clothes!" Brad scowled at a kid whose pants were rolled into skinny cuffs. "He should have just let them bunch up at the bottom. And he could have left the shirt untucked."

Nana and Mom exchanged smiles, but said nothing.

"What's going on?" asked Jill, coming in from the family room. She narrowed her eyes at the pile on the table. "So that's where my *Ursula's Unmentionables* went . . ." She picked up the catalogue and leaned over Brad's shoulder.

Brad was eyeing a kid in a linen blazer. The kid's hair was so perfect that Brad wondered if they'd styled it with shellac. The blazer was buttoned at his waist and the kid was wearing a polo shirt under it, with the collar snugly closed. "Look at this stiff! Where's he going, to his own funeral?"

Jill made a tsk-tsk sound with her tongue. "Where are the Fashion Police when you really need them, huh?"

"The blazer should be unbuttoned. Definitely. And with a plain old regular T-shirt under it."

Jill gave Brad a wink and a nod of agreement. "My sentiments exactly."

Brad smiled. Nana reached over and patted his hand.

"They're going to know they picked the right kid," she said. "As soon as they see that smile."

"It's just a regular smile."

"No, honey." Nana shook her head. "There's nothing

regular about it. That's a smile that comes all the way up from your toes. It goes right to your eyes and it drags out those dimples and, I swear, it even makes your hair a little blonder."

"Good smile," said Jill.

"And," said Nana, tucking the papers under her arm and waggling one eyebrow, "if I'm not mistaken, it's also a smile guaranteed to melt little girls' hearts!"

Brad rolled his eyes. "How do you know that?"

"Because . . ." Nana began.

"Because it's your father's smile," Mom finished, grinning. "You've got your father's smile, Brad, and you'll just have to take my word for it when I tell you, it's definitely a heart-melter."

Brad gave her the smile without even trying.

Mom went back to her coupons and Nana lugged the flyers back to the recycling bin. And Jill, when no one was looking, very casually handed the lingerie catalogue to Brad.

She wasn't exactly the big brother he'd always wanted. But sometimes she came pretty darn close.

CHAPTER FOUR

"Holy Cow, I Think He's Gonna Make It!"

At 12:39 on Saturday afternoon, Brad practically tumbled out of T.J.'s car and sped across the driveway, taking out several innocent branches on his rush through the hedge. He was in and out of the shower in three and a half minutes. He brushed his teeth, ran a comb through his hair, and stopped moving only once—to admire that morning's game-winning ball, which he'd placed dead-center on his dresser, next to a framed snapshot of him with his dad.

Mom was waiting in the car. "Brad. Your hair."

He got in the front seat. "What about it?"

"It's still wet."

"I know. I'm gonna stick my head out the window."

"Oh no you're not. That's dangerous." She reached across him to push open his door and gave him a nudge.

"Get in the backseat. It'll be plenty windy back there."

Brad got out and got in again. His mother started the car and backed out of the driveway, and Brad let the wind pummel him.

"How was the game?" Mom asked through the breeze.

Brad smiled, seeing that final play in his mind like an instant replay. "Well . . . since you ask . . ."

Brad's team had been leading 5 to 2 going into the ninth.

There were only two problems. One was that they were going into the ninth at ten past twelve. The other was that suddenly Nicky Gambini was off the mound and behind the dugout, barfing his guts up.

("That's what happens," Bernie Klemp had observed, "when a guy scarfs down three chili dogs between innings!")

"Brad," Trev hollered. "Let's go."

But T.J. was already at the corner of the dugout, waiting to drive the relief pitcher home. "I was just about to . . ." Brad stammered, "I mean, I gotta . . ."

"You gotta crush Skeff," Trevor supplied, thrusting the ball at Brad. "That's what you gotta do."

"Trev, I . . ."

"Play ball!" Bernie ordered. "C'mon!"

So at twelve-fifteen the relief pitcher took the mound. He clutched the ball and waited for the batter to step up to the plate.

The kids in the bleachers got so quiet that the only

sound was poor Nicky sprawled out in the grass, groaning behind the dugout. Out of the corner of his eye, Brad could see T.J. holding his wrist up and tapping his watch in warning. As if Brad needed any warning.

His team was ahead, so he knew if he could strike out the next three batters, they wouldn't have to finish the inning. He could get his butt home, change, and go smile for the birdie on time.

"Okay, fellas," he'd muttered under his breath, "we're gonna have to make this quick."

Brad still wasn't sure where that first pitch had come from—maybe it was the thought of going off to model that just sort of scared it out of him. But he'd wound up and fired the ball and it sailed past the batter, who looked as if he hadn't even seen it coming. The ball hit the catcher's mitt like thunder; Trevor actually wobbled in his stance.

"Strrrr-iiiiike!" cried Bernie Klemp, not even trying to hide his surprise.

His second pitch was a masterpiece of a curve, and the third, another fast ball, almost caught fire in Trevor's glove. It all came as something of a shock to the hitter, to say nothing of the pitcher.

"Out!" announced Bernie, as Trevor lobbed the ball back to Brad on the mound.

The second batter stepped up. No fooling around now—Brad held his glove against his gut, the ball behind his back, and lunged forward, staring down the batter.

Trevor stood, stepped to the right of the plate, and raised his mitt, advising an intentional walk. The kid was a hitter.

But Brad shook his head. He could guess what Trevor was thinking: *C'mon, Wilson. Don't get cocky now.*

Trevor raised his mitt again. *C'mon, Wilson. Walk 'im.*

Brad shook him off. *No time to argue, Trev old pal. Gotta pitch the ball. Gotta throw the strike. Gotta model school clothes.*

Trevor went back to crouch behind the plate. Brad wound up.

The ball came like lightning and struck Trevor's mitt.

Bernie gave a little backward jump. "Strike!"

The batter swung at and missed the next two pitches.

Bernie shrugged. "See ya'."

Then Skeff was up. Brad adjusted his cap. He shook out his throwing arm.

"Whatdya doin?" shouted Skeff. "Waitin' for your nails to dry? C'mon. Pitch the ball."

Brad gave Skeff his fiercest stare . . . *It is very unprofessional to be late for a shoot* . . . He hurled the ball.

Skeff got a piece of it. It rose in a high arc over first and came down in the grass outside the first-base line.

"Foul ball!" cried Bernie. "Strike one."

Trevor ran over to get the ball, then brought it out to Brad.

"Skeff's a jerk," said Trevor. "Don't let him get to ya'."

Brad took the ball and stared at it.

"By the way," said Trevor, "did I mention I spoke to Jessie this morning?"

Brad's head snapped up.

"Yeah. And she asked me to tell ya' somethin'."

"What?" Brad momentarily forgot Skeff was awaiting a pitch. "What?"

Trev grinned. "I'll tell ya' . . . right after you smoke a couple of strikes past Parker, I'll tell ya'."

Brad punched the ball into his glove and smiled. The teammates high-fived each other, and Trevor jogged back to home plate. He squatted and threw down the signal.

Brad wound up and tossed in a good clean strike that whizzed past Skeff's midsection.

Skeff snarled.

"Strike two!"

Trevor tossed the ball. Brad caught it, wrapped his hand around it, and prepared his fingers to work their magic with a killer curve.

All he had to throw was one more strike. His heart raced as he went into his windup . . .

And then from the stands came Pamela Hartley's voice: *"You're a babe, Bradley!"*

Crap! Brad's thumb slipped, his fingers buckled, and the ball released itself in a pitch that looked nothing at all like a killer curve. It didn't look like a knuckleball. It didn't look like a fastball, either.

What it looked like was a pitch Skeff Parker could actually *hit!*

And the ball hit the bat as the bat hit the ball, and the sound was an almost perfect whack that sent the name-less pitch sailing backward in a long, low line.

Skeff dropped the bat . . .

. . . Trevor pushed his mask onto his forehead . . .

. . . Bernie took a gallop sideways to get a better look . . .

. . . Skeff Parker sprinted for first . . .

. . . And Brad Wilson *dove!*

He dove, springing from both feet, stretching his arm out, reaching . . .

. . . reaching . . .

. . . *Pfffummph!* The ball's flight ended where it began—in the soft safe pocket of Brad's glove.

Trevor let loose with a "Yeah, baby!"

And Bernie Klemp used the strength of every muscle in his body to jerk his thumb backward. "Yerrrrrr owwwwwwwwt!"

And at the halfway point in the first-base line, Skeff stopped running. For once, he did not need to be told twice. Because Skeff had seen the pitcher diving, reaching, grabbing that ball right out of the atmosphere—he'd heard it come to rest in Brad's worn, well-oiled glove. And the perfection of it, the justice of that catch, had simply stopped him in his tracks. Skeff hadn't deserved to touch that base, not after a grab—a miraculous grab—like that one. And he knew it.

But he wasn't about to admit it.

"You got lucky, Wilson!" Skeff shouted.

Nobody bothered to answer him . . .

". . . And that's the play-by-play," Brad concluded. The scene melted away in his mind, like game footage on the evening news. He could see his mother's eyes in the rearview and could tell she was impressed. He remembered the way the players on both teams had been shaking his hand. He closed his eyes now, trying to recapture the electric pleasure of the crowd around him, wanting to congratulate him.

"And what was the message from Jessie?" Mom asked, braking for a stoplight.

"Oh . . . well . . . There wasn't one, actually."

In the rearview, Brad could see Mom's eyes crinkling. "Good thinking, Trev," she said, smiling.

"Yeah," said Brad, and he smiled, too.

Brad's hair was completely dry when they reached the photo studio. Dry and windswept. He caught a glimpse of himself in the rearview mirror. *Very* windswept. He remembered Plaster-Head in the linen blazer, and decided Ms. Heinz was going to hate it.

Crossing the parking lot, Brad felt butterflies starting in his stomach. He was heading toward a modeling shoot, for Pete's sake! Weird. The kid who just caught Skeff's screaming line drive and won the game was heading for a modeling shoot.

He followed his mother through a door and up a stairwell. The building sure didn't look glamorous. At the top of the stairs was a fire door; they pushed through it into a very bleak corridor.

"Are you sure this is the place?" asked Brad.

Mrs. Wilson consulted the directions Ms. Heinz had provided. "This is the place." She stopped at the fourth door and in they went.

Inside was another world. The room was vast—high and wide, and filled with people and equipment. There were lights on tall poles, and lights on the floor. There were tripods, like the one Brad had seen in the Home Entertainment Department at Baker's, but these stands were not holding any puny handheld camcorders—no, sir. These tripods were balancing complicated-looking cameras with lenses that resembled cannons, or telescopes. Wide-angle and zoom lenses, Brad figured, which could capture a shot of someone smiling on Jupiter.

There were also tall poles with what looked like upside-down umbrellas perched on top. The umbrella things were shimmery-white and silky-looking. People were aiming lights at them, then checking something with meters they held in their hands.

They raised the meters up to enormous backdrops— white ones, black ones swirled with gray, bright blue ones speckled white. Some of the backdrops were pulled taut and smooth; others hung loosely, bunched and wrinkly, like sheets right out of the clothes dryer. These tall, vertical backgrounds dropped to a loose crease near the floor, where they continued on, like a carpet, sprawling their colorful illusions over the studio's wooden floorboards.

There were the usual ridiculous school-related props—giant textbooks and pencils, a blackboard, one humongous apple for the teacher. (The apple was the size of a boulder; Brad could only imagine the teacher!)

Against one wall Brad spotted a long, rolling rack hung with clothes—all of them perfectly pressed and just the right size for a thirteen-year-old boy.

And then he spotted the thirteen-year-old boys.

There were nine of them, and all with the Look. Each, of course, had his own variation of the Look. A couple were blond, like Brad, but with different haircuts. Four had very dark hair, but of the dark-haired ones, no two had the same color eyes. There was an Asian kid whose skin was a rich bronzy-gold against his jet-black hair. There were two African-American guys. One was tall and very slender and wore his hair in a buzz cut. The other was on the shorter side; he had huge liquid-brown eyes.

Ms. Heinz appeared then, rushing around at a very businesslike pace. "Bradley—right on time. Good, good." She looked at him and her eyes widened. "*Love* the hair!"

This caught Brad off guard. She was looking at him and he could almost see the wheels turning in her brain. A girl with a hairbrush approached him as if he were the enemy, but Ms. Heinz stopped her.

"No! No, don't touch. He's perfect. He's divine, just as he is. That hair is an inspiration." Ms. Heinz was circling Brad, studying him as if he were a museum piece. "The style, or shall I say the lack of style—it just screams freedom, doesn't it? It's so fabulously unconcerned, so deliciously disheveled. So *genuine!*" She flicked a finger through Brad's bangs and squealed. "Whose fabulous idea *was* this?"

"Mine," said Brad.

Ms. Heinz turned and gave two sharp claps. "Quickly, boys, quickly. Mess your hair, please. Mess it up!"

The boys obeyed, looking both shocked and happy. In seconds there was not one straight part in the bunch.

Ms. Heinz turned back again and smiled at Mrs. Wilson. "You're welcome to stay and watch."

Mom scanned the studio. Brad could tell she was checking to see if any other moms were hanging around; none were. He had a hunch she would have liked to stay, but was relieved when she said, "No, I think I'll be going."

"That's fine." Ms. Heinz shook Mrs. Wilson's hand and fluttered off, leaving Brad and his mother alone.

"Go get 'em, champ," she said, squeezing his shoulder. "You'll be dynamite."

"Thanks." Brad gave his mom a grateful smile, then whispered, "Don't kiss me, okay?"

"I wouldn't dream of it."

Brad watched his mother cross the busy studio and

make her exit. Then he turned, took a deep breath, and headed toward the rest of the models.

"How ya' doin'?" he said, and hoped they couldn't tell he was nervous. "I'm Brad."

They all said hello and introduced themselves. To Brad's surprise, it felt a little like the beginning of a sandlot ball game. He was starting to feel more comfortable.

"Have any of you guys done this before?" he asked.

The answers varied. Four had modeled for Baker's. Two of them had actually done TV commercials. The rest were rookies, like Brad.

One of the boys who'd done commercials, Cody, asked if he had a skateboard.

"Not with me," Brad told him.

"No problem," said another. "We'll get a break later on, and we usually go out and ride. You can use one of ours."

Brad couldn't believe it. "Cool."

The photographer joined them then. "Okay, men," he said, shaking some hands, patting some shoulders, and smiling around the group. "Ready to get to work?"

Brad was surprised to see that the photographer was hardly older than T.J.; he seemed like a friendly, laid-back kind of guy. Brad had been expecting someone more offbeat, more artsy, dressed from head to toe in black, cranky, temperamental, barking orders at everyone. But this guy seemed all right. He was wearing blue jeans, a neatly pressed denim shirt, and an expensive-looking necktie. He could have been your social studies teacher, or something.

"We've got a nice easy session planned," the photographer said.

The models who'd been there before gave him a good-natured laugh. The photographer laughed, too.

"I know, I know! There's no such thing as an easy shoot, right?" He clapped a hand onto Brad's shoulder, grinning. "Well, we're gonna do our best to get you men in and outta here fast. It's too nice a day to be stuck inside. We should all be out fishing or shootin' hoops!"

Brad returned the photographer's grin.

"By the way, for you newcomers, my name's Marty."

The studio began to click into action. A young woman herded the models over to the clothing rack and, with a careful eye, began handing out shirts, sweaters, and pants. From time to time, she'd consult a clipboard. Once she yelled over her shoulder, "I need footwear!" as if she were a medic calling for plasma.

Then the rookies followed the veterans toward a curtained area, where they changed their clothes. For the first couple of seconds, Brad was miserably self-conscious, but Cody said, "It won't seem so weird if you think of it like a locker room." And he was right.

Brad pulled on the shirt of his first outfit, a green-and-white-striped button-down, and automatically began rolling up the cuffs.

Cody gave him a friendly grin. "I wouldn't do that if I were you," he advised. "They like us to wear the sleeves down, buttoned at the wrist."

"But I never wear my sleeves like that."

"Neither do I," said one of the other kids.

"You're gonna have to button the top button, too," said Cody, with a look that told Brad he didn't understand it, either.

"And if they give you high-top sneakers," said a tall, dark-haired kid, "they're actually gonna make you *tie* them!"

Brad scowled. He remembered the geeky kid in the ad circular. He was about to *become* the geeky kid, unless he did something to save himself.

The hair episode had proved that Ms. Heinz was open to new ideas, so he kept rolling his sleeves and soon noticed the others watching him with admiration. After a moment's hesitation, Cody pulled a blue polo shirt over his head; he did not adjust the collar or fold it neatly into place—he left it just the way it landed and didn't even bother to tuck the shirt into his trousers.

When the models emerged from the "locker room," it was *not* as the pressed and pleated platoon Ms. Heinz had described back in her office. This was a bunch of high-spirited, comfortably dressed boys with their sweater sleeves pushed up, their shirt collars rumpled, and their untied sneakers gaping open around their bunchy socks.

Ms. Heinz blinked.

The wardrobe girl looked as if she might faint.

And Marty laughed out loud. "It's about time!" he said, smiling.

Ms. Heinz's eyes had begun to sparkle. "You?" she asked, pointing to Brad. "Your idea?"

Brad shrugged. "It wasn't an idea, exactly," he admitted. "It was just me . . . getting dressed." He shoved his rolled shirt sleeve up a bit. "Is it okay?"

"Okay?" cried Ms. Heinz. "It's *fabulous!*"

(He should have known.)

The first shot featured Brad, Cody, and another kid—Joseph—and the huge apple. Marty told them to just stand in front of the wrinkled white background so he could get a light reading.

An assistant held the meter thing up to Brad's chin and said, "Good," so Marty snapped a couple of black-and-white Polaroids. When the Polaroids developed, Marty showed them around and everyone agreed they were ready.

The assistant with the meter must have noticed that Brad looked curious. "Take a look," he said, offering the curled photographs to Brad. "This is just to make sure there aren't any huge shadows or anything."

"And to make sure nobody's fly is down," added Cody, laughing.

The assistant was nice. He told Brad he could keep the Polaroids if he wanted to, to show his family.

"Here we go," said Marty, lining himself up behind the camera on the tripod. He leaned down and pressed his eye to it. "You guys, just be natural. Hey, somebody tell a joke!"

Joseph told one. It was pretty good and the boys laughed. Marty snapped some shots.

"Hands in your pockets," someone suggested. *Snap, flash.*

"Hands out of your pockets," said someone else. *Snap, flash.*

"Blond kid—lean against the apple."

Brad winced, then leaned against the apple.

Marty raised his head from behind the camera and looked at Brad. "The apple?" he asked, as if on a hunch.

Brad stepped away from the mutant fruit and laughed. "Stupid," he said, truthfully. "Corny."

"That's what I thought," said Marty, nodding. Politely, he ordered that the prop be removed.

The guy who'd given Brad the Polaroids rolled the apple away and cracked, "Anyone for turnovers?"

It was a pretty dumb joke. Brad laughed and rolled his eyes, and Marty said "Great!" and started snapping.

"Smile." *Snap, flash. Snap, flash.*

"Don't smile." *Snap, flash.* "Excellent."

Then the clothes girl was scooting Brad and the other two boys away from the white backdrop and telling one of the commercial kids and two of the dark-haired guys to take their place.

Brad went back to the "locker room." His second outfit was a gray sweater and a pair of khakis. He decided to tie the sweater around his waist and this time he rolled the sleeves only about an inch above his wrists. When Ms. Heinz saw him, she beamed. He was told to stand against the blue-speckled backdrop.

The guy who'd rolled the apple was dragging in the giant pencil for this shot. He stopped but did not put the pencil down. He looked at Brad expectantly, which was when Brad realized that Marty, Ms. Heinz, and the assistants in the studio were looking to him for an opinion.

"Uh . . . well . . ." Brad shoved one hand in his pocket and stroked his chin with the other.

(Snap, flash.)

"It's worse than the apple," he said matter-of-factly. "But if we used it to . . ."

Marty was nodding eagerly as Brad explained his idea, and in a matter of minutes the new shot had been set up. Two of the taller models—one clutching the huge eraser, the other shouldering the blunt tip, were holding the pencil between them. And in the middle Brad, with his shirttail dangling, was pumping out a series of chin-ups!

He wasn't sure but it seemed as if Marty used an entire roll of film on that shot alone.

After that, there were a bunch of shots Brad wasn't in at all. He stood with Joseph and watched the other guys get photographed. They didn't even have to be quiet; Brad thought that was a big plus. He found out that Joseph was a swimmer and that he was training for the Olympic trials. Brad was totally impressed.

The only downer was when (before Ms. Heinz could

intercede and explain about the new, genuine, unconcerned hairdo) a girl with blue lipstick spritzed Brad with hairspray. She wanted to dust him with beige face powder, too, but Marty stepped in just in time, to say it wasn't necessary.

After some shots of Brad and another guy arm-wrestling (Brad's idea) atop a four-foot-tall science book, Marty said, "How about a break?"

And the next thing Brad knew, he was outside, rumbling over the blacktop on a borrowed skateboard, watching as Joseph and Cody practiced jumps on a makeshift ramp in the middle of the parking lot.

They talked about paychecks, and girls, and the Yankees' last win, and girls, and some kid somebody knew who broke his collarbone playing street hockey, and girls.

Then the girl with the blue lipstick was poking her head out the door, telling them to come back to work.

Work? thought Brad, flipping the skateboard up and into his arms. *This isn't work!* What it was, was one of the best days of his life.

CHAPTER FIVE

The Rookie's on Deck

That night at supper, Brad could not stop talking about the shoot—the props, the cameras, the photographer, the clothes.

"They thought you were a genius for rolling up your sleeves?" Meggie giggled, passing a plate of leftovers. "Jeez. Those people should get out more."

Brad scooped up a helping of mashed potatoes. "They were the same dorky outfits they always advertise, but we managed to desissify 'em . . ."

Aunt Jill smiled. ". . . And they looked great on you?"

"I didn't say that!"

"But you were *thinking* it!" said Meggie.

"All right, all right . . ." Mrs. Wilson reached over and disarmed the tablespoon full of peas Brad was aiming at his sister. "I'm sure Brad did look great in the clothes he modeled. After all, that *is* the point, isn't it?"

Brad studied his potatoes a moment. "Doesn't matter, anyway. That stuff they made us wear—it probably cost a fortune."

"Well," said Jill, pouring Brad more lemonade, "you did earn a nice chunk of change today. I think you *should* treat yourself to something incredible."

Brad would never admit, even to his aunt, that the thought had crossed his mind. But this money was going toward helping out with the household expenses. He leaned back in his chair and shook his head. "What the heck would I do with a closet full of expensive clothes?"

"I wasn't suggesting a whole designer wardrobe, Brad." Jill sipped her lemonade. "But a few classic pieces are always a sound investment."

Brad changed the subject. "The other models and me . . ."

". . . and I."

"The other models and *I* . . . we went skateboarding during the break. It was cool. One of the guys is gonna swim in the Olympics. Two of them have even been in TV commercials."

This impressed everybody, even Meggie. Brad said he didn't know which commercials the guys had been in, or when, so Meggie made some guesses—she'd narrowed it down to either the one for the cereal that turns your milk purple or the Band-Aid commercial where the kid on Rollerblades scrapes half his knee off, when the phone rang. She went into the family room to answer it.

"So, Brad . . ." said Nana, picking up the platter of warmed-over meatloaf. "Do you think you'd like to do it again?"

"Huh? Well . . . uh . . ." Brad leaned forward. "Again? Hmm." He pushed some potatoes around and squashed a pea. He leaned back. "I don't know. I mean, it's not like Ms. Heinz asked me to, or anything." He shrugged. "I guess I really haven't thought about it."

"Well, you better think about it fast," said Meggie, returning from the family room. "Ms. Heinz is on the phone and she says you've got another job. *If* you want it."

Brad was out of his chair and into the family room before Meggie even finished her sentence.

"Hello?"

"Hello, Brad. Am I interrupting?"

"No, no. It's fine. Um . . . what's up?"

"Marty and I thought you did a *fabulous* job today! *You* . . . were *born* . . . to model."

"Thanks."

"We're doing another shoot this coming Tuesday. Junior formal wear. Same hourly rate. Interested?"

Brad didn't know what junior formal wear was any more than he had known what "a big push in young men's casual" had meant. But he said, "Sounds great, Ms. Heinz."

"Divine, Bradley!" came Ms. Heinz's voice through the phone. "We'll need you to stop by the store Monday afternoon for a fitting."

"I can be there."

"Junior Formal Department. Say threeish?"

"Threeish, sure."

"Fabulous."

Brad had never heard anyone use the word "fabulous" twice in one conversation before. "Okay. See you Monday."

"See you Monday," said Ms. Heinz. "And, Brad . . . I just know you're going to be a natural in a tux!" She hung up.

Brad returned to the kitchen. The women stared at him.

"Well?" said his mother.

"I took the job," said Brad. "It's Tuesday."

"Congratulations!" Jill raised her lemonade glass. "Hey, you may wind up being the world's youngest male supermodel!"

"Oh, I don't know about *that,*" said Brad, giving his aunt a modest shrug. "But I do know one thing."

"What's that?"

"*I'm* gonna be a natural in a tux."

After lunch Monday, Brad told his grandmother he was heading down to Baker's.

"So early?" said Nana.

"Yeah," said Meggie, who was still eating her baloney sandwich. "I thought you said you had to be there at three."

"Not three," Brad corrected her. "Three-*ish*. Threeish

is not three. It's maybe a little after, maybe a little before."

Meggie checked the clock. "Not two and a half *hours* before."

Brad threw her a look. "First of all, it is very unprofessional to be late, okay? And second of all . . ." He didn't feel like giving his sister the second-of-all.

"That's fine, Brad," said Nana. "Your mother will pick you up on her way home from work."

Brad took off through the screen door. Behind him, he could hear Meggie in the kitchen, saying something to Nana about the Ego That Ate the World.

He decided to walk to Baker's rather than ride his bike, because he didn't want to be all sweated up for his fitting. He'd never worn a tuxedo before. He'd never actually *wanted* to, but for some reason, all of a sudden, he was really looking forward to it.

Walking toward Baker's, Brad felt strangely confident. He felt grownup. The fact that earning money would finally make him the man of the house was certainly part of it. But there was more, some feeling he couldn't exactly describe: Special? (Too goofy.) Important? (Possibly.) Babelicious? (Definitely. But he didn't want to dwell on that one.)

He kept checking his reflection in store-front windows, curious to see if he looked as confident as he felt. He did.

When he reached Zowalski's News and Variety, a block before Baker's, he went inside.

"Hi, Mr. Z.," said Brad, heading for the magazine section.

From behind the counter, Mr. Zowalski waved, and said, "The new *Sports Illustrated* just came in!"

But when Brad turned the corner into the aisle of magazine shelves, he walked right past the one with the latest issues of *Sports Illustrated, Wrestling World, Car and Driver,* and *Baseball Digest.* He passed the business monthlies, too, and the home and garden magazines. He even went right by the comic-book display and didn't stop until he reached the section he was looking for.

The fashion magazines.

There were a ton with glamorous women on their covers, but only a few featuring men. Brad scanned those four covers, then reached for the one that looked the most masculine—the magazine's title was *GQ.*

Brad took the book from the shelf and studied it. The picture on the cover was of a young man in his mid-twenties wearing a tank-top undershirt and dressy slacks, looking like maybe he hadn't finished getting dressed and someone accidentally took the picture. The undershirt showed off his muscles. He had a mass of dark hair, slicked back, and the kind of sideburns Brad thought had gone out of style. The guy wasn't smiling.

Brad opened the magazine. The first fifteen pages were advertisements. There were cologne ads, and razor ads, and ads for suits from Italy, and every one of them featured a guy in his twenties who wasn't smiling. Some looked happier than others, but they managed to do it with some expression that didn't exactly fit the text-book definition of a smile.

Brad wondered if these guys went out skateboarding during breaks.

He looked from page to page, from model to model, and decided he had never seen so many dimples in his life. Dimples, but no real smiles. To Brad, the models all looked as if they had just been yelled at—or as if they had just met the girl of their dreams. Or as if they had just been yelled at *by* the girl of their dreams. They all had scowly, pouty, growly looks on their faces.

Brad glanced up at the shelf to check the faces of the women on the other magazine covers. Most of them were smiling, but a few did look as if maybe they had just been yelling at some sideburned guy in his twenties with dimples.

He flipped a few more pages of *GQ*. There was a black-and-white two-page ad for jeans. Same muscular, rugged-jawed type of guy; same mop of smooth slick hair. And no smile. This jeans guy had sort of a part grin, part snarl on his face. Personally, Brad wasn't crazy about the facial expression, but he was sure that this guy, both pages' worth of him, was getting paid a lot of money for—what would you call it, anyway?—*grinarling* like that.

Brad studied the photo. He pushed his hair back, hoping it would stay, like the model's did. But it came sweeping down again into his eyes.

Then he tried to *grinarl*—to grin and snarl at the

same time. He knit his eyebrows slightly and bit down hard on his back molars, sucking in his cheeks. He willed his own dimples to appear, but doubted they would without the aid of an actual smile. Then he concentrated on getting just the corners of his mouth to curl up, while puffing his lower lip out (like Meggie used to do when she was younger and about to burst into tears).

He held the face and went to look in the mirror Mr. Zowalski kept near the tall rack of inexpensive sunglasses.

Not even close.

He relaxed his face and took another look at the magazine's cover.

Then he tried to imagine getting yelled at by Jessie Brock, and looked in the mirror again.

Much better!

The hair was still wrong of course, but maybe the girl with the blue lipstick would have something to help that. He held the expression a moment longer, until he heard someone say his name.

"Bradley?"

He turned away from the mirror fast. Jessie was standing behind him.

"Hi, Jessie." He tucked the magazine behind his back.

"Trying on sunglasses?" she asked.

Brad shook his head.

"Oh." She gave him a brilliant smile, then turned and started browsing the lipstick samples.

"Trying on lipstick?" he asked. "Cause if you are . . . I wouldn't recommend blue."

"Blue lipstick?" Jessie shook her head. "No, I'm not allowed to wear makeup yet. I just like to look sometimes."

"You don't need makeup," he said, before he could stop himself.

Jessie smiled again, bashfully this time. "Thanks. That's sweet of you to say."

She picked up a pale pink lipstick for a closer look. While she was doing that, Brad slipped the *GQ* onto a countertop, under a pile of newspapers.

"So what are you up to?" Jessie asked, returning the lipstick to its display.

Brad wasn't about to tell her he was off to try on tuxedos. Saturday's shoot had been fun, but he still wasn't planning to go public with this modeling thing. "I have to go to Baker's," he said vaguely, because he couldn't bring himself to lie to Jessie.

"Really? Me, too."

"Cool," said Brad. "I'll walk you there."

On their way out, Mr. Zowalski gave them one of those silly mushy smiles grownups give kids the first time they're spotted walking with a member of the opposite sex. Brad tried out his model face on Mr. Zowalski—he gave the storekeeper what he hoped was a friendly "grinarl."

Mr. Zowalski raised his eyebrows. Brad took this to mean that his model face needed some work.

"I like to start school shopping early," Jessie explained, as they walked off in the direction of Baker's. "I go look at the stuff and decide what I want, so when it gets marked down later, I don't have to waste time trying things on." She laughed. "You kind of have to work fast at those back-to-school sales! It's every girl for herself, if you know what I mean." She gave him another bashful smile. "I really love clothes, so I'm sort of fussy. And this way, I'll know exactly what to pick out when the sale starts."

"August 14," said Brad, without thinking. "The fourteenth to the thirty-first. Forty to sixty percent off Baker's entire stock."

Jessie tilted her head. "How do you know?"

"Uh . . ." Brad could have kicked himself! "Lucky guess."

He kept his mouth shut for the rest of the walk.

When they reached the fancy glassed-in entrance to Baker's, Jessie said, "I guess you're on your way to Sporting Goods, right?"

"I guess so." Then he added, "Actually, I might check out Young Men's Casual. I wanna invest in some classic pieces." *That* should impress her.

"Really." She looked more surprised than impressed. "Well, thank you for walking me."

"Thank you for letting me walk you."

"See you later."

Brad watched as she walked away toward the trendy

Juniors Department. As far as he was concerned, there was really no reason for Jessie Brock to try on school clothes, because he already knew how every outfit was going to look on her—*fabulous*!

Between Young Men's, Home Entertainment, and Sporting Goods, Brad was able to kill the remaining time before it officially became threeish. At two forty-five, he took the escalator to the third floor. Junior Formal Wear was cramped into a far corner. That made sense to Brad—how much demand could there be for this stuff? Tuxedos for thirteen-year-old boys. Brad hadn't even known they existed.

"Excuse me . . ." he said to a white-haired gentleman with a yellow tape measure draped around his neck. "I'm here for a fitting."

The man nodded. He looked as if he should have some stuffy English accent. But he didn't. "Are you a ring bearer?"

"A ring bearer? No, I'm . . ."

"No, no, no," said the man, "of course not. You're too old to be a ring bearer. You must be a junior groomsman."

"No, I'm not."

"Are you an usher?"

Brad was confused. "An usher?"

"Yes." The man seemed to be getting impatient. "Are you an usher? In a wedding party."

"No," said Brad. "I'm a model. In a sales circular."

"Oh, of course!" The man snapped the tape measure from his shoulder. "You must be Bradley."

Brad nodded. "Ms. Heinz said threeish."

"Very good, very good. Nice to meet you, Brad. I'm Edward."

"Hi."

Edward took some straight pins from a cushion on the counter behind him. "Shall we get started?"

Brad watched as Edward put the pins in his mouth. It seemed a pretty stupid, not to mention dangerous, place to keep pins.

"Do you know your inseam, Brad?" asked Edward. "I'm thinking twenty-three, twenty-four maybe."

"Is that like my social security number or something?"

Edward laughed. The next thing Brad knew, there was a tape measure running from his crotch to his ankle.

"Hey . . . is this necessary?"

"Yes, actually."

Brad stood perfectly, *perfectly* still. In seconds, Edward had moved out of that area and on to Brad's waist. Brad guessed that taking inseam measurements was probably the worst part of the guy's job.

Next, Edward wrapped the yellow tape around Brad's chest. After that, he measured from the shoulder to the wrist. He wrote everything down on a pad.

"Good proportions," Edward said. "Not much to do at all."

As long as there was no more inseam nonsense, Brad would be happy.

Edward disappeared for a moment and returned carrying a garment bag with a Baker's logo on it. He handed the bag to Brad, then pointed. "Take this into the fitting room over there and try it on."

Brad headed for the fitting room. Inside was a three-way mirror, and in front of it was a round, carpeted platform about ten inches high. Brad hung the garment bag on a hook, unzipped it, and got his first real up-close look at a tuxedo.

He couldn't help smiling. He felt like James Bond!

At least, he felt like James Bond until he tried to put the thing on. He doubted very much that Agent 007 ever had trouble dressing himself. Brad, on the other hand, was lost. He stood there in his underwear, struggling with each separate tuxedo component, like some kind of idiot.

Nothing looked familiar, nothing was *regular*. The pants had buckles on the sides, the vest had no back to it, and the buttons on the shirt were so tiny he couldn't get his fingers to work them. The sleeves were nine miles too long. They looked as if they were supposed to get folded up, but when Brad tried, he couldn't get them to stay there.

"Uh . . . little help here, Eddie."

Edward came in, still chewing the straight pins. Unfortunately, Ms. Heinz was with him. Brad reached down to his ankles and pulled the pants up, fast. How many of these underwear incidents was he going to have to endure, anyway?

"What seems to be the problem?" asked Edward.

"I just don't get it," said Brad. "Tuxedos should come with instructions."

"Oh, but they come much better than that!" cried Ms. Heinz, sweeping her arm toward Edward. "They come with tailors!"

Edward told Brad to stand on the carpeted platform, then adjusted the waist of the pants so—to Brad's great relief—they stayed up on their own. Next he knelt down and tugged at the pant legs a little, folding up the bottoms and sort of pinching them, so there was a nice firm crease where they broke over Brad's toes. The tailor looked to Ms. Heinz for approval.

"Perfect!" declared Ms. Heinz.

So Edward began plucking the pins from his mouth one by one. He had the hems pinned up in no time. Then he stood and buttoned the shirt with such ease, coordination, and lightning speed that Brad silently dubbed him a fashion athlete. In mere seconds, the backless vest was a perfect fit.

The bow tie was next, and it wasn't one of those cheesy clip deals, either. Edward stood behind Brad and positioned the tie under the shirt collar. Then he wrapped, threaded, and tugged until there was a flawlessly tied bow nestled comfortably under Brad's chin. All that remained to repair were the sleeves, which were still flapping around, hanging to Brad's knees.

"Cuff links!" barked Edward, and Ms. Heinz ran out, then ran in again, carrying a little velvet box. She handed them over to Edward, who took them like a surgeon accepting a scalpel.

Edward opened the box.

"Diamonds?" Brad couldn't believe it. He held his breath while Edward fitted them into the holes in the shirt's stiff cuffs.

"*Voilà!*" said Edward.

Brad looked at himself in the mirror. "Wow!"

"The Look!" cried Ms. Heinz. "You see what I mean? I knew you'd be a natural!"

Brad had to admit it—he was. He tried his scowly pouty growly face. And this time it worked.

"Shoes!" Edward marched out and returned holding a pair of shiny black shoes. They were so shiny Brad wondered if Edward had oiled them, like a baseball glove.

"Patent leather," Ms. Heinz explained. "Tuxedo shoes are always patent leather. Don't you love them?"

"Well . . . um . . ."

"You can be honest," said Ms. Heinz. She gave him an understanding look. "I want you to be honest, Brad, because if a model is not comfortable with what he's wearing, if he is not spiritually one with his ensemble . . . well, it can compromise the innate truthfulness of the shoot, detracting from the tone and quality of the photos, ultimately degrading the integrity of the entire concept of fashion as we know it."

Brad looked to Edward for a translation.

"She's saying the pictures will stink if you hate your shoes."

"That's exactly what I'm saying!" cried Ms. Heinz. "So you *must* tell me, Bradley, honestly. *Do* you like these imported, hand-crafted, extremely expensive tuxedo shoes?"

"Not really. I mean"—he wrinkled his nose at the shoes—"they look slimy."

"Slimy?"

"Kind of." Brad shrugged. "They'd be okay for a grownup, I guess. But in real life a kid would never wear those."

Ms. Heinz looked at the shoes. Then she looked at Edward, who nodded.

"He's right, you know," said Edward.

Ms. Heinz smiled. "Of course he's right. This kid is a *kid*! He's the genuine article." She turned back to Brad and opened her arms. "So then, Brad. Tell me. Honestly. What kind of shoes *would* you wear?"

Brad didn't even hesitate. "Spikes," he answered.

"Spikes?" said Ms. Heinz.

"Yep." Brad nodded.

"You'd wear baseball spikes with a tuxedo?"

"Ms. Heinz," said Brad, grinning, "I'd wear baseball spikes any chance I got! And my cap too, for that matter. I mean, as long as I'm being truthful."

Ms. Heinz stroked her chin and began pacing the fitting room. "So you're saying in all honesty that, given

the option, you—an actual thirteen-year-old actual *boy*—
would choose to wear baseball shoes with a tuxedo."

"In all honesty, I probably wouldn't even wear a
tuxedo." Brad shrugged. "But if I had to, say if I was
going to be a gloomsman or something . . ."

". . . that's *grooms*man," Edward corrected, smiling.

"If I had to wear a tuxedo in real life, I'd just feel better about the whole thing if I were wearing my spikes
and my cap with it." Brad finished with another shrug.
The diamond cuff links were reflected like sparks in the
mirror, shooting off tiny trembling prisms all over the
room.

Ms. Heinz was smiling. "So we'll do it! We'll put you
in baseball shoes. Baseball shoes with a tuxedo! It's brilliant! It'll lend reality, frivolity, and above all *honesty* to
the entire campaign. Oh, Bradley, you're a genius! A genius."

A genius who has the Look and who is a natural at becoming spiritually one with a tuxedo, Brad almost reminded her. But then he decided it wasn't necessary to
say it.

Why bother? It was written all over his face.

CHAPTER SIX

A Real Team Player

Tuesday's formal-wear shoot was nothing like the one for young men's casual. The shoot for young men's casual had included young men (other than Brad), and the whole thing—the studio, the atmosphere—had been very casual. But junior formal wear was another story. There was only one other guy model for Brad to hang around with, and the mood was as far from casual as it could get.

The photographer, Bernard, was wound tighter than the string inside a baseball, and for reasons Brad could not quite identify, Bernard wanted everyone to speak in whispers. His assistant had a bad summer head cold and her ears were so clogged that she missed half of what everyone said.

The other guy model was some creep named Porter

Dickson, and within five seconds of being introduced, Brad had silently nicknamed him Plastic Boy. His hair didn't move, his clothes didn't wrinkle, and, unless the camera was aimed directly at him, his face didn't have any expression at all. Porter's formal wear consisted of a blazer called a dinner jacket—it was white and clean, and Brad half imagined that if Porter wore that jacket for the rest of his life, it would remain as spotlessly pristine as it was today.

Brad decided to keep his distance.

The shoot was taking place in what Ms. Heinz called a "location house," a private home that had been rented to Baker's for the afternoon. Brad couldn't imagine anyone living in this place, but Ms. Heinz assured him that someone did. The entire crew were nervous wrecks, tiptoeing across priceless carpets and being careful to keep the hot, powerful lights aimed away from irreplaceable oil paintings and wall tapestries.

Oh, and there was the girl.

Her name was Cass. That was it—just Cass. "For professional purposes," she told Brad, "I've dropped my last name."

"Well, if I see it," Brad joked, "I'll pick it up for ya'."

He laughed. Cass didn't.

She was wearing a strapless gown that must have been designed by Cinderella's fairy godmother. She had eight or nine coats of gloss on her lips and false eyelashes that made her look as if two tarantulas were sleeping on her eyelids.

"It's really *en vogue* in the industry now for models to go by just one name. Like Miranda. She's on all the runways. She's done everyone's collections. And she only goes by one name. Haven't you ever heard of Miranda?"

"Miranda who?" cracked Brad. He laughed. Cass didn't.

But she was a stunner, all right.

"How old are you?" Brad asked, just to make conversation during a break.

"Fourteen and a half," said Cass.

Brad was going to guess twenty-three. So much for conversation.

Not that he could have come up with anything else to say if he'd wanted to. Brad was having a tough time concentrating; he kept sneaking glances at Cass. She caught him once and pretended to be annoyed, but after that, she started doing things that made it impossible for Brad not to look.

Like sighing. She had this really breathy sigh, which ended in a sort of moaning sound. Not the miserable moaning sound Nicky Gambini had made following the chili-dog incident, either. Cass's sound was kind of nice.

And stretching. Not *just* stretching, but rolling her shoulders and pressing her ribs outward, and reaching her arms up so high that her strapless gown had a difficult time staying where it belonged.

And checking her nylons. She'd slip the skirt of her gown up indecently high, extend her leg slowly, then bend her knee and rest her foot on a chair to examine the condition of her hosiery. Brad tried to get a reading—not exactly nude, not quite suntan, and definitely not panty hose. Cass's hose stopped at a lacy band near the top of her thigh.

She caught him looking again and he gulped.

"Nice shoes," he managed.

She sighed.

Walk it off, Brad told himself. He wondered what the feminine equivalent of *babelicious* was.

But, all in all, he was having a pretty good time. His tux looked great with his baseball cap and spikes. At first the crew was having a heart attack about Brad wearing spikes on the imported Venetian marble floor. But Ms. Heinz had reasoned, "These tiles outlived the Roman Empire. I think they can handle a pair of baseball shoes."

That was one of Brad's favorite parts of the day.

They all loved Brad's growly, grin/snarl non-smile. Cass especially loved it.

Once she'd seen it, he caught *her* sneaking glances at *him*.

He also got high praise for coming up with the spikes idea. Apparently, "reality," "frivolity" (whatever that meant), and "honesty" were big with these people. One guy even said that "putting spikes together with a tuxedo implied the underlying struggle between man's destiny to grow old and his futile desire to recapture youth." The guy also said the look was refreshing; "refreshing" was the only word Brad understood.

For six hours, he cheesed it up for the camera in the big, fancy rooms of the house, and outside on the lush green lawn. He goofed around with his cap a lot—brim in front, sideways, backwards—and Bernard took pictures with the hat in each position. They took some without the cap, too, and to Brad's disgust, they insisted he wear hairspray for those shots, since it was crucial that his hair stay properly unkempt.

Plastic Boy tried desperately to keep up with Brad. When Brad ran, Porter ran; when Brad jumped, Porter jumped. But where Brad's moves were agile and natural, Porter's were stiff and awkward. When Brad wowed everyone by pulling off his spikes and socks and shinnying up one of the ancient Grecian porch columns, Plastic Boy tried to compete by hurdling over a wrought-iron patio chair.

Bad call! Porter's pants cuff caught on the arm of the chair and Porter went skidding across the slate floor, scraping a nice patch of skin off his forehead.

Brad had been scraped worse than that a billion times in his life and hadn't so much as asked for a Band-Aid. But Plastic Boy cried like a baby, screaming for iodine and plastic surgeons, and, most important, a mirror.

Needless to say, Porter was relieved of his dinner jacket. Reality was one thing, Ms. Heinz explained—a bloody forehead was quite another. He wouldn't be finishing this shoot, and unless he had a remarkable capacity to heal, he wouldn't be getting called for any others for a while, either. Brad knew from experience, when a wound like that scabbed over, the crusty stuff could hang on for weeks.

At the end of the shoot, Ms. Heinz handed him an envelope. "Your first paycheck," she said. "Saturday's earnings."

"Thank you." Brad decided it would probably be bad manners to open it in front of her.

"I'll be in touch," said Ms. Heinz. Then she shook his hand and walked away. Her heels went clicking across the Venetian tile.

Brad held his breath, opened the envelope, and looked at the check. It was made out in his name and it was for more money than his mother earned in two weeks. He couldn't believe it—for some reason, it made him almost as sad as happy. Then he heard Ms. Heinz coming back across the tile.

"I almost forgot to tell you, Bradley. I've seen the contact sheets from the back-to-school shoot."

"How'd they come out?"

"Fabulous! Even better than we'd expected. And *you* stole the show!"

Brad felt proud to hear that. It seemed almost too bad, though. Since he was never going to tell anyone that he'd modeled, none of his friends would ever see the shots. It almost bothered him. Almost. But the bottom line was that he wanted this to be his secret forever.

"Beyond fabulous," Ms. Heinz was saying. "So fabulous that we've decided to do something very special with one of them."

"Special?" Brad wasn't sure he liked the sound of that. "You mean like put me on page one of the circular or something?"

Ms. Heinz laughed and it didn't sound as rusty as it had in her office. "You're thinking small, Bradley. Think big . . . big . . . *big!*"

"How big?"

"Well, how does forty-eight feet by fourteen feet grab you?"

"Beg your pardon?"

Ms. Heinz took both of Brad's hands in hers and squeezed them. "We're putting you on the billboard!"

"Billboard? What billboard?"

"The one near the Middle School! Perfect for our target audience." Ms. Heinz laughed again. "Isn't that just fabulous, Brad? Did you ever in your wildest dreams imagine that you'd be on a billboard?"

"Never," he answered glumly. "Not in my wildest dreams."

But at the moment Brad's wildest dreams were the furthest thing from his mind. Because, at the moment, he was living his worst nightmare.

He was about to hit the billboard again. But he had a feeling that this time Skeff Parker wouldn't be impressed.

When Brad flopped into the recliner, he was shaking. He picked up his father's scrapbook; it seemed to weigh a thousand pounds in his hands. He grabbedfor the pen and started writing like mad.

"Wilson Hits Billboard—This Time, Face First! Baseball Career Over—Social Life Comes to Humiliating Halt." Brad punched the air in frustration.

He was only supposed to be in some stupid little flyer. They were gonna stick him between the comics and the coupons in the Sunday paper, and nobody but a bunch of old ladies he never met were gonna look at it. Nobody ever said anything about the billboard, for Pete's sake! How could this happen?

Brad leaned back hard in the chair. A sliver of sunlight filtered through the small window; long shadows, cast by the trophies, stretched across the cellar.

"I don't care if Joe Namath *did* wear panty hose once," he told himself out loud. "*He* didn't go to Haverton Middle School. *He* didn't have to deal with Skeff."

Brad heard the sound of gentle laughter. He sprung forward, opening his eyes.

"Mom?"

She was standing in front of him, holding a box of old clothes.

"I didn't know you were home," she said, setting the box down. "How was the shoot?"

Brad pretended not to hear the question. "What were you laughing at?"

"Oh," said his mother, "I was just trying to imagine Skeff Parker bullying Broadway Joe." She chuckled again. "I mean, picture it."

Brad did, and it actually brought a smile to his face. "Pretty ridiculous," he admitted.

Mom took a seat on an old rocking chair. "So what about the shoot?"

Brad shrugged. "It was fine. Except . . ."

"What, honey?"

He decided he might as well tell her. She'd know soon enough, anyway—the billboard was a pretty hard thing to miss.

"Ms. Heinz says Baker's wants to feature me on the billboard. The one by school."

"Bradley!" Mom's eyes went wide. "Oh, sweetie, I'm so proud! That's . . ." Then it registered. "Ohhhh. I see the problem."

"So much for keeping this modeling thing a secret, huh?"

Brad's mother reached over to stroke his hair; it didn't move. "Are you wearing hairspray?"

"They made me." He grabbed his bangs and tried to mess the spray out of them. "Mom, I don't want anyone to think I'm some stuck-up glamour boy. I don't want them to think I'm a sissy for modeling clothes."

Mom lifted an eyebrow.

"But does it make me a sissy to be so *afraid* of people thinking I'm a sissy?"

She shook her head. "Nope."

"All I wanted to do was take care of you and Meggie," said Brad. "I wanted you guys to think of me as the man of the house."

His mother gave him a curious look. "You think seeing you on the billboard is going to make us think differently? I want you to listen to me," she said, taking his chin in her hand. "Really listen, okay?"

Brad nodded.

"The real you is what's inside. And before you start rolling your eyes at me . . . I *know* it's an old cliché. But it's the truth, sport. Really. That gorgeous kisser is just what the gods decided to wrap you up in." She fluttered her eyelashes comically. "You look just like your mother!"

"Yeah, well, we use the same brand of hairspray."

"Ha, ha." Mom rolled her eyes at him. "I just want you to realize that modeling is nothing to be ashamed of, or embarrassed about. Would you feel this way if Ms. Heinz had offered you—oh, say, a paper route? Or a job cutting grass somewhere?"

"No. But cutting grass isn't sissy junk."

"Neither is modeling. And you know it. Just as a man shouldn't judge himself by how he looks, he also shouldn't judge himself by what he does for a living. As long as it's honest work, and as long as he does it to the best of his ability."

Again, Brad nodded.

Then Mom narrowed one eye at him. "And while we're on the subject, mister, let's talk about this whole 'man of the house' thing."

"What about it?" said Brad.

"I think it's sweet and generous of you to want to help

out, but I hope you haven't gotten the idea that supporting a family is a gender-related trait. It has nothing to do with being a man, Brad. It has to do with taking responsibility and caring for people. It's not about being male or female—it's about being an adult."

Brad sighed.

"All right," said Mom, "I'm off the soapbox. But the point I want to make, Brad, is that as much as we appreciate your unselfishness, no one expects you to be an adult—not yet. All you have to be right now, champ, is a kid. Just a kid."

"A kid on a billboard," Brad reminded her, dourly.

For two weeks, Brad had trouble sleeping. Every time he'd close his eyes, he'd see himself, two stories high, smiling down over the Haverton ball field. He actually stopped by Ms. Heinz's office once and tried to persuade her to change her mind. No such luck.

He couldn't eat. His stomach was flipping constantly, as if gymnasts or rodeo clowns were practicing inside him.

The only thing he *could* do was play baseball. Ironically, his unwelcome modeling success seemed to give way to some very welcome baseball success. The anxiety pulsed through him and released itself in the form of fastballs and RBIs.

He'd meet his friends at the diamond and pitch a season's worth of unhittable curves. Then he'd pick up a bat and send line drives blazing through the infield, or fly balls sailing fast and furious toward the very same billboard that, in a matter of days, would have his face plastered across it.

For two weeks, Brad stunned his teammates. But Skeff Parker was always there to remind him that he still hadn't managed to hit the billboard again, and the challenge was still on.

Brad would grumble, "Yeah, yeah," and keep swinging.

Of course, none of Brad's friends could understand why he wasn't thrilled with himself. He'd seemed happier when he was just an average player, and that made no sense at all.

Ms. Heinz had explained that the billboard would go up very early in the morning, two days before the back-to-school sale was scheduled to begin.

"Customers will get to admire your face for an entire forty-eight hours," she'd told him. "They'll see you, adore you, want to *be* you! Or at least be *like* you. They'll stare up into those bright larger-than-life green eyes and ask themselves, 'What must I do to become like him? Ah, yes. It's so simple—I must go to Baker's and buy clothes . . . and electronics, and sporting goods, and housewares—and then—*then* I shall be like him. Like Bradley. Like the Great and Powerful Bradley of the Billboard'!" Ms. Heinz gave him a glowing smile.

"That's brainwashing," said Brad.

Ms. Heinz had said, "That's *advertising*."

Brad wondered what the difference was.

He was still wondering on the morning of August 12, when he crept out of the house at 5 A.M.

The neighborhood was silent, the sky a glossy lavender. Brad had never been outside this early before—the world seemed to have entered a different dimension. The sliver of moon he remembered from the night before had slipped toward the horizon. It looked milky against the morning sky. The air was cool and damp.

He rode his bike through the quiet streets toward school. Only a few cars passed; they had their headlights on. A newspaper truck screeched to a stop in front of Zowalski's store and left a stack of papers on the sidewalk. Somewhere, folded into that pile, was the Baker's sales circular. Somewhere in there was Brad's picture.

Part of him wanted to rifle through the pile of papers to see it.

Part of him said, "First things first."

Pedaling toward the field, Brad could see the billboard guys already at it. He leaned his bike against the backstop and walked out to the mound. He sat down on the rubber, drew his legs up, and wrapped his arms around his knees to watch.

The men worked quickly, expertly. Behind the sign, the sky had begun to brighten. The dampness in the air was giving way to mid-August heat. The sound of traffic increased—car horns, squeaky brakes, and rattling mufflers echoed across the outfield.

Brad watched in awe as his image emerged on the sign. It was one of the shots Marty had snapped when

Brad was laughing at the dumb apple-turnover joke. He was wearing the striped shirt, and he had one hand sort of half in and half out of his pocket. There was something very natural about the pose, and it looked as if he was having a *fabulous* time. He had a playful smile on his face that looked nothing like the grinning snarl, snarling grin he'd learned from studying the jeans model in *GQ*.

And then the men were taking down the scaffolds and packing up their truck. The billboard was complete—just in time to dazzle the drivers in the morning rush.

Brad stood slowly, studying the enormous rendering of himself that now stood beyond center field. He was filled with some weird feeling not unlike the feeling he'd get on the day school portraits were passed back—times ten million. On picture day, kids went around peeking at other kids' pictures, asking, *"How'd yours come out? How'd yours come out?"* And somebody always had his eyes closed and would have to get it redone.

But that picture-day feeling wasn't just curiosity, or excitement, or even relief (when you turned out not to be the kid with his eyes closed). The word to describe that feeling, and this one, was a word Brad heard Aunt Jill's soap-opera characters using all the time: *vulnerable.*

Because, on picture day, there you were, close-up, in full color, for everyone to see. You could only hope you didn't have something disgusting stuck to the end of your nose, or a big zit bulging out of your chin. Or maybe they'd notice that the dress-up shirt you'd worn for picture day this year was the exact same dress-up shirt you'd worn for picture day last year, because you couldn't afford a new one. And there you were: vulnerable.

And here he was now—bigger than life, for everyone to see. Ms. Heinz said they would adore him. But what if they didn't? What if everyone in Haverton noticed that his left eyebrow was a fraction of a millimeter longer than his right? What if they thought his lips looked a little chapped? What if they thought he was stuck-up, conceited? Or worse, what if they didn't think anything at all?

Brad blinked at the billboard. He could lie—maybe Skeff Parker was stupid enough to believe the model on the billboard was actually Brad Wilson's long-lost evil twin . . . Not a chance. (That wouldn't even work on the soaps.)

He stood a moment longer, watching as the morning sun shone in his billboard eyes, lighting up his billboard hair. Then he turned, got on his bike, and pedaled home.

What else could he do?

The phone started ringing halfway through breakfast.

"Is that Bradley on the billboard?" Nana's bridge partner wanted to know.

"I just saw your boy," Mom's boss called to tell her, "and he's twenty feet tall!"

"His teeth look terrific" was what Dr. Washburn, their dentist, had to say.

Nana had bought ten copies of the newspaper; on the kitchen table were ten copies of the circular, opened to the Young Men's Casual page. Mom couldn't quit saying how handsome Brad looked, and Meggie developed an instant crush on Cody.

T.J. stopped by to congratulate Brad, and Jill poured him a cup of coffee. The phone rang again, and this time Brad got up to answer it himself.

"Hello?"

"Wilson?" It was Trevor. "Tell me I'm nuts!"

Brad sighed. "You're not nuts, Trev."

"*Man!* What the heck are you doin' on the billboard?"

"Laughin' at a dumb apple-turnover joke," Brad answered flatly. "Who else saw?"

"Just Scott. We went to the field early so he could practice bunting."

"What did he say?"

"He said, 'Trev, come with me to the field early so I can practice . . .' "

"No! What did he say about the *billboard*?"

"Oh. He said the same thing I said: 'Holy cow. Brad Wilson's on the freakin' billboard, man.' That's what he said."

Brad dragged his hand down his face hard. He figured Trevor would be busting out laughing any second, so he braced himself. But the laughter didn't come.

"So how'd you get on the freakin' billboard, man?" There was a hint of admiration in Trevor's voice that Brad was surprised to hear.

"Well, I just sorta got offered the job."

"Job?" Trevor sounded amazed. "You mean they paid you?"

"Yeah."

"How much?"

Brad told him.

"Jeez, Wilson! Are you the luckiest kid on the planet or what?"

Lucky? Brad wasn't sure if Trevor understood that being paid to appear in a billboard advertisement officially made a guy a model. "You think I'm lucky?"

"Sure! You're gonna be famous." Trevor gave him a respectful chuckle. "I mean, you were already practically famous for hittin' that billboard with a fly ball. Now you're gonna be twice as popular for gettin' your mug up there. It's like the world's biggest baseball card or something."

Brad cleared his throat. "Ya' think?"

"Heck, yeah!"

Brad couldn't believe it. The word "sissy" hadn't come up once. "So, we gonna play later?"

"There's a game kickin' up at two."

"Cool. I'll see ya' there."

"Okay. Oh . . . Brad . . . one more thing."

"What?"

"You know that shirt you're wearing on the billboard? Do you happen to know if it comes in blue-and-white?"

Brad smiled. "Yankees colors!"

"You know it, man!" Trevor laughed. "So . . . uh . . . does it?"

"Yeah, Trev. I think so."

"Cool."

Brad hung up the phone, stunned and happy. It rang again almost the second he put it down. He snatched it up quickly.

"Brad looks great on the billboard!" came Pamela Hartley's voice through the wire. She giggled a little before she hung up.

Brad grinned, returning the phone to its cradle. For once, he and Pamela were in complete and total agreement.

CHAPTER SEVEN

He Goes Down Swinging

Brad could not get to the ball field fast enough. And yet he felt as if maybe the best thing he could do was not show up at all.

He arrived on time. Crossing the grass toward the backstop, he could see his friends standing around home plate, looking up at the billboard.

"Hey, guys."

They all turned at once. Each face was a mix of shock and curiosity.

Brad shrugged. "It's no big deal."

"Trev says they paid you a fortune," said Scott.

"Yeah, sorta."

But before anyone else could ask a question, they heard laughter coming from the curb. Again they turned, this time to see Skeff arriving. Brad should have known; it was an evil laugh.

"Look at this!" Skeff bellowed, passing the bleachers.

"The Glamour Boy goes Big Time!" It wasn't a compliment.

"Back off, Skeff," said Trevor, but Skeff kept laughing.

"He's a model, a *freakin'* model!"

"So?" said Norman, tossing a ball up and catching it in his mitt. "So Brad's on the billboard. So what? Let's play ball!"

The others agreed.

"C'mon, let's play."

"Choose up sides already."

"Let's play ball."

But Skeff wouldn't quit. "Did they make you wear lipstick, Miss Bradley? Did they put eyeshadow on you, too?"

"No." Brad clenched his teeth. "Cut it out, Skeff."

"I bet you won't be hittin' that sign anymore, will ya'? I mean, you wouldn't wanna mess up your pretty picture!"

"Back off, Parker," said Trevor.

"Or get lost," added Scott.

Skeff gave them a disgusted look. "So you guys are actually gonna let the pretty boy play? I mean, c'mon! I've never heard of no model playin' sports."

"Sure they do," offered Bernie Klemp. "They do commercials. Sneaker endorsements, and that kinda stuff."

"Sneaker endorsements ain't modeling!" insisted Skeff. He waved his arm at the billboard. "I've never seen any pro athlete with that kind of stupid smile on his face. And check out the clothes!"

"What's wrong with the clothes?" asked Trevor.

But Skeff had made his point. Some of the guys were laughing now, and whispering, and Brad knew he was losing ground.

"Are we gonna play baseball or what?" said Scott.

"Yeah," said Skeff. "We are. And if you want Gorgeous George, you can have him."

They picked teams quickly and took their positions. Brad was about to throw the first pitch when he heard Skeff taunting him from the bench.

"Remember, Wilson," he roared, his voice ricocheting off the cement walls of the dugout. "It isn't whether you win or lose, it's how pretty you look when you play the game."

Brad pitched. The ball rolled off his fingertips, weak and wobbly.

"Ball one," said Bernie.

It was going to be a long inning.

Around the fifth, the world began to darken. Clouds drew together in a looming gray mass. The morning's heat burned off to a cool gloom, and from somewhere far off, the sound of thunder drummed in the sky.

Brad was stepping up to the plate for his third at bat when the rain started—long, fast drops that sliced down, leaving a random pattern of small circles in the dirt.

"That's the game!" cried Bernie Klemp.

"Huh?" Brad spun to face the umpire. "You're calling the game *now*? The rain just started."

Bernie shrugged. "In twenty minutes, there's gonna be

no visibility and the field's gonna be a big muddy mess."

"So wait twenty minutes," Brad reasoned. The rain was picking up, but not enough to call the game. "The baselines aren't even wet yet!"

Bernie gave Brad a weird look. Then he called "Game!" again and walked away.

Grumbling, the outfielders headed for their dugout. On the mound, Skeff was having a conniption fit.

Brad dropped his bat into the rain-spattered dirt and hurried after Bernie.

"Bern, man, what are you doin'? We could play another twenty minutes! What are you doin'?"

Abruptly, Bernie stopped walking and turned to face Brad. "I'm savin' your butt!" he said in a whisper. "That's what I'm doin'. Your first up, you fouled out. Your second, you hit the most pathetic grounder I ever saw and then didn't beat the throw."

"Yeah, but . . ."

"Yeah, but if you get another up, you're probably gonna pop out and make Skeff's life, okay? I can't let that happen, man. I can't let you go down in flames."

A fat raindrop hit Bernie on the nose. He wiped it with the back of his hand and left a muddy smear. "Last week, you played serious baseball. You played like my old man says your old man used to play—like a legend. But Skeff got you riled about the billboard, and now you're playing like garbage." Bernie shook his head slowly, a gesture of respect and heartbreak. His whisper was more urgent when he said, "Be glad this game is over. I'm tellin' you, Wilson, I'm savin' your butt."

Bernie turned to continue walking, just as an enormous flash of lightning ripped through the sky. Seconds later, the thunder. The rain came faster, more furious now, and the ball players ran for their bikes, or for their moms' cars, which always seemed to appear magically whenever the weather turned.

Brad stood in the downpour, soaking up Bernie's words as his shirt soaked up the rainwater. *Everybody has an off day,* he told himself. He personally had never had *such* an off one before, but he had heard that even legends foul out now and then.

He squished through the mud toward the dugout to grab his glove. Then, squinting into the rain, he began the long, wet walk home. He stopped at the curb to glance over his shoulder at his picture. He happened to do this at the exact same moment that another flash of lightning electrified the sky. It reminded him of the flash of Marty's camera. Brad turned and kept walking.

His second concern was that this heavy rain might damage his baseball glove.

His first concern was for the billboard.

The clothes dryer was running, so no one heard Brad coming in the door to the laundry porch. He was drenched, and miserable. He peeled off his sopping T-shirt and dropped it into the washing machine. Then he kicked off his spikes and yanked off his muddy socks. He was so grumpy and preoccupied that he had actually stripped down to his underwear before he even noticed there were people sitting at the kitchen table. He peered in through the window.

Mom, Meggie, and Jessie Brock.

Jessie Brock!? He immediately dropped to his knees on the linoleum. Brad's misery changed to terror. There was only one way into the house from the laundry porch—and that was through the kitchen. Through the kitchen in his underwear, to be exact.

Thunder exploded outside. It seemed to be asking: *What is Jessie Brock doing at your kitchen table?*

Brad didn't move.

"I can't imagine what's keeping him," Mom was saying. "They never play in this weather. My sister-in-law borrowed my car today, or else I'd have gone down to the field to pick him up."

Great, Mom, thought Brad from the floor of the porch. *Make her think I'm a total baby, why don'tcha?!*

"I hope he gets home soon," said Meggie, sliding a plate of cookies toward Jessie. "I wanna see the look on his face when he finds you here. He might die of happiness right before our eyes."

(Brad made a mental note to cut his sister's hair off in her sleep.)

"Actually," said Jessie, "I can't stay much longer. I have a ballet lesson this afternoon."

Brad had all he could do to keep from jumping up and shouting, *"Don't go!"* Then a better idea struck him: he opened the dryer door. The clothes stopped tumbling and fell into a warm pile inside the drum. Brad dug into them, searching out a pair of shorts and a sweatshirt.

Unfortunately, though, the clothes in the dryer belonged to Aunt Jill, and even more unfortunately for Brad, this particular load consisted exclusively of delicates—silky panties, nightgowns, and lingerie.

In the kitchen, he could hear Jessie saying goodbye.

His heart raced. *What do I do, what do I do?* It was life or death, now or never. If he didn't get in that kitchen fast, Jessie was going to leave.

So Brad Wilson did exactly what any other red-blooded American boy would do in such a desperate situation—he reached into the dryer, pulled out a pink satin bathrobe, and wrapped it around him.

"Hi," he said, stepping into the kitchen.

Mom, Meggie, and Jessie turned. Mom's mouth dropped. Meggie burst into hysterics. Jessie smiled.

"Hi, Bradley."

"Hi, Jessie." He clasped his hand around the knot in the satin belt and walked as carefully as he could toward the table. When he reached the chair, he sat down fast.

"What are you wearing?" Meggie giggled. "Did your team get new uniforms?"

Mom bit back her own laughter and tried to give Meggie a threatening look.

"I got stuck in the rain," said Brad. "This was in the dryer."

"Once, on vacation," Jessie offered, "my suitcase got lost and I had to wear my brother's clothes for the whole trip."

Meggie rolled her eyes. "A perfect couple," she mumbled.

Then Mom excused herself and dragged Meggie out of the kitchen with her.

When he and Jessie were alone, Brad asked, "What's up?"

"I just wanted to tell you I think the billboard is terrific."

Brad felt his face flushing. He wasn't sure if he was flattered or embarrassed or just feeling the heat of the fresh-from-the-dryer satin. "Thanks."

"I didn't know you were a model."

"Neither did I, till some lady at Baker's told me I was."

"You should be very proud of yourself."

Brad took a cookie from the plate and shrugged. "I should be. I'm not sure if I am, though."

"Why not?"

"The guys were sorta giving me a hard time about it. Skeff Parker said I was a wuss."

"That's ridiculous," said Jessie. She placed her hand on the pink sleeve of the robe. Then they both glanced at the satin fabric, raised their eyebrows, and cracked up.

"I just hate having Skeff rank on me," Brad admitted.

Jessie stood up and said matter-of-factly, "Skeff is jealous."

Jealous. Brad wasn't sure how to respond to that. So he just smiled.

"My parents are having a cookout this Saturday," said Jessie. "I was wondering if you'd like to come?"

Brad's eyes widened. "Sure." Then a dark thought hit him. He remembered the way Cass had gotten all dreamy-eyed after she'd gotten a load of his model snarl, and how she wouldn't leave him alone.

"Uh . . . Jess?"

"Yes?"

"You're not just askin' me cuz of the billboard, right?" As soon as he said it, he knew he shouldn't have. Thunder rumbled through the sky.

For a moment, Jessie looked hurt. Then she gave him an understanding smile. "No, I'm not asking you because of the billboard. But I guess I can see why you might think that."

"I'm sorry," said Brad, and he meant it. "That was a crummy thing to say. I know you're not like that." He stood cautiously. "Am I still invited?"

"Of course you are," said Jessie. "And just for the record, I was going to ask you anyway, even before the billboard."

"Really?"

"Yes, really." Now she was blushing. "I was going to ask you that day you walked me to Baker's. But I chickened out."

"Oh."

They stood there smiling at each other awhile. Finally, Jessie said, "See ya'."

"Yeah, see ya'. I'd walk you to the door but . . ."

Jessie laughed. "That's okay. We wouldn't want anyone on the street to get a look at you in that outfit!"

He heard her on her way through the family room, pausing to thank his mother for the cookies. After Mrs. Wilson had seen Jessie out, she came back to the kitchen, where Brad was still standing, with a happy, dazed expression on his face.

"She's a sweet girl."

Brad nodded. "She invited me to a cookout."

His mother smiled. "You really are becoming quite a young man."

And even though he was wearing a pink satin bathrobe, Brad knew it was the truth.

The next morning, Brad awoke to noise outside his window. The noise was followed by a tapping sound. *Probably more rain,* he told himself, *or a demented squirrel.* He rolled over toward the window and opened one eye.

Then he sat bolt upright!

It was not some demented squirrel tapping on his windowpane. It was girls. *Girls!* Hundreds, maybe thousands! Seven, at least—huddled around his window, waving and giggling like numskulls!

Brad pulled the sheets up to his chin! For one crazy second, he thought about calling for help. For another crazy second, he scanned the floor of his bedroom, just to make sure he hadn't left his jock strap lying around with the rest of his dirty laundry. (Girls watching you sleep was one thing; having them see your jock was another!)

Then his bedroom door banged open and Meggie appeared. "Is this crazy or what?"

"What's goin' on? Who are they?"

"Pamela Hartley and her creepy crew."

"Oh, man! Why are they here?"

"Well," said Meggie, taking a seat on the edge of the bed, "I think they're your fans."

Brad turned back to the gaggle of girls pressing their faces against his window. One of them blew him a kiss. He turned back to his sister. "You gotta be kidding!"

"They showed up about an hour ago," Meggie explained. "At first, they were just kinda hangin' around on the sidewalk, staring at the house. Then I got this great idea."

Brad frowned. "I'm not sure I wanna hear this . . ."

"I told them, for one dollar—*each*—I'd show them where your bedroom window was." Beaming, Meggie pulled seven bills out of her pocket.

Brad slapped his hand to his forehead in disbelief. "Has everybody around here gone completely nuts?"

"They paid a buck to see you sleep," said Meggie. "Yeah, I'd say they've all lost their marbles!"

Brad and Meggie looked out at the girls. Then Brad realized something.

"Meg?"

"Yeah?"

"Did you give them a time limit or anything?"

"Darn!" Meggie snapped her fingers. "I didn't think of that." She looked at her brother. "Why?"

"Because . . . I gotta go to the bathroom!"

Meggie laughed. "So get up and go."

"I don't want the Heartless Wonder to see me in my pajamas!" Brad sunk into his pillow and covered his head with the bedding. Maybe they'd get tired of looking at his old blue-and-gray-striped sheets and go away.

He waited a long moment. "They gone?"

"Nope. Still there."

"Meg . . . !"

"Okay, okay."

Brad could feel the bed spring upward as Meggie hopped off.

"What are you going to do?" he asked from beneath the covers.

"I'm gonna tell them their one-dollar time is up. If they wanna keep looking at you, they're each gonna have to cough up another two-fifty!"

Brad lowered the sheet to expose one eye. "Two-fifty?"

"Yeah!" said Meggie. "Like they say on those phone-psychic TV commercials. 'Call the Astrological Pals Network. A dollar for the first minute, two-fifty for each additional minute.' "

"What if they pay it?" asked Brad, worried. He hadn't wet the bed in ten years and he sure didn't want to have a relapse in front of seven giggly girls.

"Nobody would pay three dollars and fifty cents to see a lump of covers," Meggie reasoned, "when they could go down to the ball field and look at you on the billboard for free!"

Brad listened as Meggie crossed the room and left. He stayed hidden, trying to keep his mind off his bladder, until she returned and announced, "The coast is clear!"

"Finally!" said Brad.

When he got back from the bathroom, he found three dollars and fifty cents in the middle of his neatly made bed. He pulled on some shorts and stuffed the money into his pocket. Then he grabbed a polo shirt and headed for the kitchen, where he found Meggie at the table, buttering toast. His grandmother was cutting grapefruit.

"Morning, Nana."

"Well, if it isn't the local celebrity!" She placed half a grapefruit in front of Brad, handed him the sugar bowl, and gave him her mischievous grin. "What has this world come to," she cried out, in make-believe disgust, "when young ladies come creeping around at the crack of dawn to peek into a boy's window!"

"Weird, huh?" Brad spooned out a grapefruit section, sprinkled sugar on it, and popped it into his mouth. "I wonder how long this kinda stuff'll last."

"Probably until you get ugly," guessed Meggie.

"What makes you think I'm gonna get ugly?" Brad dug out another piece of grapefruit. "I've got the Look. I'll probably always have the Look." He did not realize until after he'd placed the pulpy pink section onto his tongue that he'd forgotten to sugar it. The tart bitterness stung him and his whole face puckered.

Meggie wrinkled her nose. "Oh, yeah. That's the Look, all right."

"What are ya', jealous?"

"I didn't mean that you were gonna get ugly," said

Meggie. "What I meant was, well, anything can happen."

Brad lowered his eyebrows. "What do you mean by that?"

"Didn't you get hit in the chin with a baseball last summer?"

"Bad hop," said Brad. His jaw ached just remembering it. "So?"

"So," said Meggie, finishing her toast. "That ball just missed your bottom lip. Mom said so, remember? She said it would have split it and you'd have gotten stitches and a scar and everything."

Brad remembered how Plastic Boy had crashed and burned.

"And what about the time Scott Treeler slid face-first into third and busted his nose?" Meggie folded her arms across her chest. "I've seen you slide, Brad. Coulda been you."

She had a point. Brad held up the grapefruit half and squeezed some juice into his mouth. "So I won't slide anymore."

"Skeff Parker could always aim one of his stinky fastballs at your head! Bam! Right between the eyes, and the next thing you know . . . two shiners for the price of one."

Brad considered that very real possibility.

"I think we should all kick in a little cash," Meggie proposed, "and get some assurance."

"I think you mean *in*surance," said Nana.

"Yeah, insurance."

"Insurance?" Brad looked at his sister. "On me?"

"Not all of you. Just your face. That way, if you happen to get your skull bashed in by a fastball, or you scrape your whole chin off during a crummy slide"— she smiled broadly—"we're covered!"

Nana took her coffee cup and headed for the family room. "This conversation is getting too violent for me."

Me, too, thought Brad. He tried to imagine his face on the billboard, sporting two black eyes. Or a broken nose. Or a busted lip. Not a pretty picture.

"Maybe you could wear a catcher's mask," Meggie suggested.

Brad got up, dumped the peel in the trash, and put his bowl and spoon into the sink. "To pitch? And to hit?" He shook his head. "That'd be stupid."

"It would be safe," said Meggie, getting up from the table. "This is the family fortune we're talking about! I just think you should take better care of it."

Brad leaned against the sink and watched her leave. Then he checked to be sure his cut of the seven bucks was still safe inside his pocket.

"Be back in a while, Nana," he called through the kitchen.

He went out the door to the laundry porch, where he nearly tripped over his spikes. They had dried up nicely from the day before. Ordinarily, he'd have cleaned them up right away, carefully removing the dirt clumps from the spikes and giving the muddy leather a good once-over with a soft brush.

Today he just kicked them out of the way and kept going.

Mr. Zowalski did something he'd never done before. He offered Brad a free copy of *Sports Illustrated* and said he could have a cold drink—on the house.

"Take your time. Look around! It's not often we get a real celebrity in here!" He took Brad's hand and shook it as if Brad were an adult. "The Mrs. and I are proud of you, son!" he said.

"Thanks," said Brad.

Mr. Z. laughed. "Maybe you should get yourself a pair of our affordable sunglasses, Brad. Celebrities always wear dark glasses—helps maintain their privacy."

Brad just smiled and nodded, then walked over to the tall cooler that held the beverages. He was trying to decide between a soda and an iced tea when he heard whispering.

"Hey, isn't that the billboard kid?"

"I think so."

"Cute!"

Brad didn't turn around. Instead, he relaxed his focus on the drink bottles so that he could see the reflection in the glass door. The whisperers were two girls standing behind him. Even in the reflection, Brad could tell they were older—probably in high school.

"Too bad he's not a little older," one whispered before they disappeared.

Brad looked around. He wished Scott, or Trev, or even

Skeff—*especially* Skeff—had been around to see that. *High school girls! Woah.* He felt light and powerful as he made his way through the aisles, stopping last at the magazine section.

At the counter, he handed his selections to Mr. Zowalski.

"The tea and the magazine are on me," the storekeeper reminded Brad, sliding those items to the side. Then he rang up the others: Chap Stick, a travel-size bottle of sunscreen lotion, and a trial-size tube of pimple cream—three things Brad had never purchased before in his life.

Mr. Z. didn't seem to notice. He put the items into a paper bag, then reached for the two freebies.

"Ooops," he said, holding up the magazine. "You must have grabbed the wrong book. This isn't *Sports Illustrated.*"

"No, sir," said Brad. "That's the right one. If you don't mind, I'd rather have that one instead."

Mr. Zowalski gave a hearty laugh. "Fine with me, son," he said, stuffing the magazine into the bag. "Least I can do for the most famous kid in town is give him a gratis copy of *Gentleman's Quarterly!*"

Brad handed Mr. Zowalski the money, took the bag, and left.

"Come again!" cried Mr. Z., waving after him.

Heading for the baseball diamond, Brad felt as if his feet weren't even touching the sidewalk.

When he reached the field, he was happy to see yesterday's rain hadn't hurt the billboard. He gave the sign a good long look and decided, for the next shoot, he was going to have the girl with blue lipstick try parting his hair differently, just for the heck of it.

None of his friends was on the field yet.

Brad opened his bottle of iced tea—he tried to do it exactly like the kids in the TV commercials opened their bottles of iced tea. The gesture was smooth, and very cool. He could almost hear the theme music in the background, as he flashed a flawless grin at a make-believe camera, then shook his hair back and took a long, performance-quality drink. One day he might find himself starring in one of those commercials, so he might as well practice.

He headed for the bleachers, took a seat, and opened the paper bag. He removed the magazine and placed it on the bench beside him. Then he took out the sunscreen and applied some to his nose and cheeks, rubbing it in carefully. After that, he smeared a few layers of Chap Stick onto his lips. It messed up the flavor of the tea, but he figured it was worth it. Then he leaned against the bleacher behind him and opened the *GQ* magazine across his lap.

In this issue, the guy from the black-and-white jeans advertisement was featured in a full-color ad for skin-care products *pour l'homme*. Brad wasn't sure what *pour l'homme* meant, but the guy's skin looked great. It made him glad he was using sunscreen (even if his travel tube had come from Zowalski's and cost only ninety-nine cents and the *pour l'homme* variety, according to the ad, could be found only at "finer department stores nationwide").

He thumbed a few pages forward and read the first paragraph of an article about tying a perfect knot in a necktie. He owned only one necktie and he rarely wore it, so he skipped ahead.

The next article was an interview with a young movie star. Brad recognized him. He'd done a really good action film last year, then got a little nuts and started doing love stories and junk. But the guy had the Look, so Brad decided to read on.

The interview was mostly about the guy getting his start in movies, but halfway through, the interviewer started asking questions about the guy's personal life. The guy said the worst part about being famous is that it gets in the way of relationships, and makes dating impossible.

Brad looked up from the magazine to the billboard. Would being famous get in the way of his relationship with Jessie?

He was still wondering when he heard voices on the field.

"Wilson, where's your glove, man?"

"Hey, Wilson!"

Brad broke through his thoughts. Trevor, Scott, and the rest of the guys were on the field. He hadn't even seen them arrive.

"He's not wearing his spikes," said someone.

"C'mon," called Trevor. "Let's play."

But Brad shook his head. "No, thanks."

Trevor looked from Brad to Scott, then back to Brad. "Ya' pull somethin'?"

Again, Brad shook his head.

"Then how come you ain't playin'?"

Brad shrugged. "I don't feel like it."

At this, everyone cracked up.

"Yeah, sure."

"Brad Wilson doesn't feel like playing?"

"Right—and I don't feel like breathing!"

Trevor smiled and rolled his eyes. "Quit jokin' around, man. Let's play."

"I told you," said Brad, tucking the magazine under his arm. He grabbed his bag from the bench, then climbed down the bleachers. "I don't feel like it."

That was when Skeff appeared. "What's goin' on?"

"Nothin'," said Brad. "I'm just not playin', that's all."

Skeff shot him a smug look. "What's in here?" he snapped, snatching the paper bag from Brad's hand to look inside. "New mascara?"

"Give it!" Brad demanded.

Skeff was laughing like a hyena as he dumped the bag's contents in the dirt. "Check this out! Billboard Boy's afraid to get his face dirty!" He kicked at the pimple cream and the sunscreen. "I guess models aren't allowed to get sunburn—or freckles."

Brad set his jaw and said nothing.

"Is that why you don't wanna play?" Trevor asked quietly, stepping closer to Brad.

Brad sighed. "Remember last year," he said softly, so

only Trevor could hear, "when I took that bad hop to the chin?"

Trevor nodded.

"And Treeler's busted nose?" Brad stuffed his hands into his pockets. "I just can't risk it, Trev. We really need the money." He decided not to mention that he also happened to *like* being a celebrity, or that high school girls would never flirt with an unknown kid with a split lip.

Trevor looked as if he understood. "The game won't be the same without you, pal."

Something in the way he said it made Brad's heart sink to his sneakers. He smiled thankfully at his friend, deciding maybe it wouldn't be a good idea to hang around and watch the game, after all.

"Maybe the wussy wimp needs to go home and get some beauty sleep," said Skeff. "Maybe all that pretty smiling wore him out."

"Shut up." Brad felt his back stiffen in defense. "Modeling's not as easy as it looks, Parker. It's hard work."

"Yeah . . ." Skeff batted his eyes comically. "I hear getting those false eyelashes on straight is excruciating!"

A couple of the guys laughed.

Brad's hands curled into fists. "I mean it. It's a tough job. Those lights are really hot and you've gotta get your clothes changed fast." As soon as he said it, he wished he hadn't. He noticed a few of his teammates rolling their eyes, disgusted.

"Awww," said Skeff, pretending to play an imaginary violin. "Poor baby!"

Brad turned to leave, but Skeff's next words stopped him dead.

"Don't you guys get it? Wilson's only quitting cause he knows he'll never hit the billboard again! And we know it, too!"

"I can do it," growled Brad. "I just . . . I just don't *wanna* do it."

"I bet you'd want to if somebody was gonna take your picture doin' it!" Skeff let out an evil howl of laughter.

Brad clenched his teeth. "Yeah?"

"Yeah!" The challenge was shining in Skeff's eyes.

In a flash, Brad snatched up a bat, which made Skeff take a quick, cowering step back. At this, Brad had to smile.

"I'm not gonna *hit* you, idiot."

Skeff recovered with a gulp. "I knew that."

"So . . ." said Brad, taking a practice swing. "Get out there and pitch already."

The other players cheered, shouting and punching their gloves in support of Brad as he stepped to the plate.

"You get one pitch, Wilson!" Skeff called from the mound.

"I only need one, Parker," Brad called back. He got into his stance, rotating the bat in small circles above his right shoulder.

But now Skeff was wasting time stretching, and unfortunately, this gave Brad a chance to think. The adrenaline pumping—not to mention the fury—was surely enough to send this ball crashing squarely into the billboard. Which was exactly what he wanted. And exactly what he didn't want—after all, this time he'd be aiming for his own face!

What if this homer dented his cheekbone, or wrinkled his chin, or tore away one whole dimple?

Skeff went into his windup.

Brad's heart pounded in his chest.

The ball came at him. He lifted his elbows, shifted his weight.

And he swung . . . He swung short and early, hitting the ball with the tip of the bat and spitting it in the direction of first base, where it landed with a muffled thud in the grass. Exactly where he had directed it.

Every eye landed there, too.

"Hah! *Hah!*" Skeff Parker fell to his knees as if his greatest wish had just been granted. "I knew it! I knew it! Whaddya call that hit, Wilson? The Supermodel Slam? I told you, modeling is for losers."

Brad let the bat roll from his grasp and fall to the ground. He wanted to scream. He wanted to cry. Tears prickled at the back of his eyes and his throat was as dry as the dirt around home plate. He felt strange and guilty, as if he'd just told some terrible lie, or betrayed a good friend.

He turned to Bernie Klemp, who'd slid his face mask up to his forehead. Bernie looked as if he wanted to cry, too, like some little kid who'd just heard there was no Santa Claus.

"I told you a guy couldn't be a model and a ball player," Skeff was gloating.

From the looks of disappointment among the others, Brad could tell they were beginning to agree with Skeff. Only Trevor and Scott, who were approaching their friend with solemn faces, seemed to realize what had really happened.

"It won't be the same without ya'," Trevor said again.

Brad gave him another grateful smile. Then Skeff hustled in from the mound, picked up the tube of pimple cream from where it lay in the dirt, and tossed it to Brad.

"Don't forget your zit zap, pretty boy!"

Brad caught it, then spun it back, like a first baseman throwing a runner out at second. "You keep it, Skeff. There's a big ugly one popping out on your neck!"

"Nah," said Scott. "That's just his big ugly head!"

Skeff slammed the tube into the dirt, and Brad turned to walk away. When he got to the curb, he glanced back and saw that some of the guys were using the abandoned sunscreen.

He watched them a moment and chuckled in spite of himself. He sure was going to miss baseball. Being rich and famous wasn't exactly a bad trade, but in his heart he knew he was going to miss the game.

CHAPTER EIGHT

Swing and a Miss

Everything changed at once.

Almost from the minute his face hit the billboard, nothing in Brad's life was the same. The local paper did a piece on him. Its headline read, *Local Looker Beautifies Billboard*. Brad clipped it out and slipped it between two empty pages in his father's scrapbook.

And the phone rang constantly, too. Most of the calls were from Pamela Hartley, who stayed on the line, it seemed, for hours. The conversations were very flirty, and mostly one-sided. Pamela talked and Brad listened.

He was beginning to think maybe she wasn't such a creep, after all.

Trevor and Scott treated him to lunch a few times at the fast-food place, and when Brad laughingly accused them of inviting him just because they wanted to watch the girls flirt with him, Trev and Scott laughingly admitted that they just wanted to watch the girls *period*. It was good for their reputations, they confessed, to be seen with the billboard guy. One day, Trev went home with the phone numbers of three different girls, and Scott got asked to the movies by a very cute cheerleader.

The next afternoon, Brad sat down with Norman, the catcher, and proceeded to give the guy unsolicited fashion advice. Brad had been pleased that the catcher had listened with such silent intensity—although Trev had commented afterward that Norm had been gritting his teeth and his fists had been tightly clenched the entire time.

"You've got good bone structure," Brad told Bernie one day, "but you've really got to drop some pounds."

Bernie had just looked at him. There had always been sort of an unspoken agreement that the guys never made fun of Bernie's weight. Even Skeff didn't tease him.

"It'll help when those stupid braces come off," Brad had added, to comfort the umpire. He didn't seem to realize that flashing his own flawless smile was almost like rubbing Bernie's face in it.

Brad never asked how the games were going, or who was batting what. Hearing about baseball only made him long for it, so what was the point? And he'd begun to assume that the guys would be more interested in being told—by *him*—how to improve their hairstyles than in discussing their stats. Brad was always happy to offer his professional opinion to his friends . . . whether his friends wanted it or not.

In spite of all the social activity, the week went so slowly that Brad wondered if God had secretly sent it into extra innings. He thought the weekend—the cookout—would never arrive.

On Friday evening, he opened his closet. Then he just stood there.

His closet wasn't exactly an inspiration. He wished he had something expensive and fashionable, but his summer wardrobe consisted mostly of nylon running shorts and sports-logo T-shirts. He had a few decent shirts but his jeans were beginning to wear out. He had one nice pair of khaki pants, but thanks to a growth spurt he'd had at the beginning of spring, they were now what his mother called "high waters."

No thanks.

He frowned into the closet and wished he owned a tuxedo. He was, after all, a natural in a tuxedo. That would impress Jessie. That would impress anyone.

Brad was still staring at his wardrobe when his mother came to tell him Ms. Heinz was on the phone. He hurried to the family room.

"Hello?"

"Bradley, darling. Fabulous news! I know it's short notice, but we'd like to use you tomorrow. Available?"

Brad bit his lip. "What time?"

"Marty wants to get an early start—say, eightish? And

he wants to shoot right in the store, instead of the studio. We're going to rope off a few areas and do the shoot for the viewing pleasure of our loyal Baker's shoppers."

Brad grinned. That sounded kinda cool.

"Should push sales through the roof," Ms. Heinz was saying. "Print advertising's answer to a live performance, you might say."

"How long do you think it'll last?" he asked. The Brocks' cookout wasn't beginning until noon.

"Hard to say," said Ms. Heinz. "I'm guessing you'll be out by eleven. Eleven-thirty at the latest."

Brad thought a moment. "Okay," he said at last. "I can do it."

"Fabulous!"

Not exactly, thought Brad, hanging up. Now he'd be cutting it close for the cookout. Still, another paycheck might go a long way toward getting some new clothes in his closet.

He went into the kitchen and told his mother about the next morning's job.

"Well," she said, placing a coffee cup on the drainboard, "I can drop you off at eight, but I won't be able to pick you up. We've got inventory tomorrow."

Brad said, "No problem," but went back to his room thinking that now he'd have to walk—no, *run*—all the way from Baker's to Jessie's house.

He took another gloomy look into his closet, then tugged his best polo shirt off a hanger. He dug his nicest pair of running shorts out of a drawer and placed them neatly in a gym bag, which he put near the door. Then he set his alarm clock for seven, flopped back on his bed, and sighed. It was a sigh that came from somewhere deep inside him.

Brad Wilson hadn't held a baseball, swung a bat, or worn a glove in four whole days. And it was beginning to cause him physical pain. His hands seemed to ache from their longing to choke up on a Louisville Slugger. His leg muscles felt tight, sore, as if he'd run for miles, when really he hadn't run at all, not even the length of a baseline. He was beginning to understand where the term "safe" had come from. There was no greater feeling of security than the sensation of his spikes hitting the bag—a feeling he hadn't experienced in days. He was lonely for baseball. And although it didn't seem like a just comparison, all he could compare it to was the way he missed—*missed,* in his heart—his dad.

And there was another nagging thought at the back of his brain, a thought that came in the form of Skeff Parker's voice:

He's quitting cause he knows he'll never hit the billboard again!

Brad curled up on his bed and socked his pillow. How could he give up and let Skeff think he was afraid? He'd let everyone down, himself especially. He *could* have hit the billboard again. Sooner or later, one would have gone screaming far and fast and furious enough to make it.

But he'd chosen not to. He'd made the decision not to risk hurting his picture. Instead, he'd thumped a pitiful, pathetic little foul ball that even Bernie Klemp could have hit.

Then again, he told himself, Bernie Klemp could never get his picture on a billboard. Bernie didn't have the Look—none of them did. They didn't have Brad's hair, his face, his smile, or his (what had Edward the tailor called them?) proportions.

So what if he'd given up on baseball? He had modeling now, and it seemed to come a lot more naturally to Brad than baseball, even on his best days, ever had. Modeling seemed to have dropped right into his glove. What was it his father used to say to describe an easy catch? "Can of corn."

Dozing off, he remembered what Trevor had said to him that last day at the field—that baseball wasn't going to be the same without Brad Wilson.

He smiled drowsily, knowing now that Trevor had missed the point. The point was that Brad Wilson wasn't going to be the same without baseball.

He was going to be better.

There was something eerie about being inside Baker's department store before it was actually open.

It was quiet and dimly lit and Brad half imagined the mannequins might come to life like well-dressed zombies thirsting after the blood of young models.

Brad would be happy when those loyal shoppers showed up.

He was wearing oversized electric-blue swimming

trunks and a tank shirt with some colorful logo on the front, and sitting on the glass top of a display case while Marty and his assistants set up lighting for the morning's first shot: Brad sliding down the handrail of the escalator. Marty was excited about this one. He explained that the motion of the model, combined with the mirrors and the metal that surrounded the escalator, would give the photos a futuristic-looking blur.

"Movement," Marty had said. "Speed. Strength."

Brad liked the idea of that. He was beginning to think his athletic ability might not have to go to waste after all, if he could apply it to modeling. Pictures requiring speed and strength could become his specialty. He thought of the muscular guys he'd seen in *GQ* and vowed to take his now casual weight-lifting routine more seriously.

Marty was loading film when Ms. Heinz came fluttering in. She looked wildly concerned about something.

"Morning, Ms. Heinz," said Brad.

Ms. Heinz just waved to him. "Where is she?" she asked Marty. "Where in the name of Calvin Klein *is* she?"

Marty shrugged, and kept loading.

Brad leaned toward Louie, the assistant who'd been making all the jokes at the first shoot. "Where's who?"

"Cass. She's late."

"Very late!" confirmed Ms. Heinz, throwing up her hands.

Brad frowned. "Isn't it unprofessional to be late?"

"Yes, technically." Ms. Heinz smoothed her skirt and shook her head. "However, it is considered very professional for professionals to behave unprofessionally."

Brad looked at Louie.

"Take my advice, kid," said the assistant. "Get out of this business while you still can."

Brad laughed. The assistant didn't.

Then there was a big commotion near the entrance, and although Brad was apparently not yet professional enough to act unprofessionally, he did understand that a commotion like this one could only mean that the professional had arrived.

"Finally!" said Ms. Heinz.

Brad watched a small entourage emerging along the wide aisle that separated the Fragrance Department from Women's Accessories. He recognized the older gentleman in the suit as Cass's manager. Behind him came Cass's personal makeup artist, her hairstylist, and then Cass.

"What, no chauffeur?" Brad whispered to Louie.

"She makes him wait in the car."

"Oh."

After Cass came another fluttery woman in a business suit (she and Ms. Heinz could have been bookends), and some raggedy-looking boy who must have been fifteen.

"The woman is Cass's chaperone," said Louie.

"Why does she need a chaperone?"

Louie shrugged. "She doesn't. But Miranda and the other supermodels drag chaperones along to Paris and Milan, so Cass drags hers here."

Brad laughed. "Who's the kid?"

"Significant other."

" 'Scuse me?"

Louie grinned. "Boyfriend."

Cass's boyfriend looked as if he hadn't slept in days, and his hair was a scraggly mop. On top of that, he looked bored and grouchy, and not at all the type he figured Cass would want to be seen with. Brad couldn't help wondering what Pamela Hartley would have to say about this guy.

His name was Ziggy. That figured.

Cass came right up to Brad and gave him a glowing smile. "Hello, you!" she crooned, leaning in the general vicinity of Brad's cheek. No actual contact was made, however. Cass planted an enthusiastic kiss in the atmosphere around his face.

Brad nodded to Ziggy. Ziggy made some snuffly grunt that Brad assumed meant hi. Then it was time to get down to business.

Cass was whisked away to change her clothes and Brad began sliding. He took a trial run down the escalator handrail, and everyone cheered when he landed on his feet.

On the second slide, Marty began snapping. The flash of the camera seemed to explode in the mirrors and metal, brilliant and blinding, as Brad zipped down the rail with his hair flying and his arms outstretched. The nylon swimming trunks made a windy sound as he slid. The tank top billowed and he was afraid he might look too skinny. But Marty and the others assured him he looked perfect.

Then Cass returned in a pair of patched denim shorts and a huge T-shirt. Her hair was pulled up in a floppy ponytail and she actually looked her age.

"Clearance!" she said in a huff. "I can't believe they've got me modeling clearance!" She walked directly over to Ziggy, spun, and posed.

Ziggy snuffled his approval—or disapproval, Brad couldn't tell. He gave his own outfit another, more critical look and wondered what Jessie would think of it. He also wondered if Ms. Heinz would let him invite Jessie next time.

He might have asked permission there and then if the stampede hadn't started.

The loyal Baker's shoppers had arrived . . . with a vengeance!

The overhead lights had just buzzed up to full blast when Brad turned to see a flood of squealing girls heading toward him from the direction of the main entrance. There were a good number of adults in the pack, but they weren't squealing. Some of them had cameras; others just looked very, very curious.

The girls were yelling to Cass that they thought she was the greatest. A fair number were calling to the "Billboard Boy."

Louie had taken a position behind one of the stanchions that held a length of velvet rope. "Here we go," he muttered.

Ms. Heinz held up her hands for silence; what she got hardly came close. "Welcome," she shouted. "Welcome to Baker's! We ask that you please keep the noise to a minimum so our models"—she swept her arm in the direction of Brad and Cass—"will be able to concentrate. Also, please refrain from using flash photography, as it will interfere with the lighting. Thank you, and enjoy the shoot."

If Cass was still annoyed about modeling clearance, she sure didn't show it. She mugged it up for the camera and the crowd, and her enthusiasm proved infectious. Soon Brad was working the room nearly as well as she was. Between shots, he shook hands with some of the onlookers. One girl tried to hug him, but Louie stepped in before she managed to get her arms around Brad's throat.

In a while, Marty directed everyone toward the Leisure Living Department to set up lights around the marked-down patio furniture. Most of the crowd made a beeline, and the assistants got moving, but Brad hung back. He hung back because Cass hung back and he thought there was something professional about that. So he hung back while the grownups, including Ms. Heinz and Cass's chaperone, disappeared through the luggage department on their way to Leisure Living.

And that was when he saw Cass throw her arms around Ziggy and give him a long, *long* kiss.

Brad felt his cheeks turn red. He'd never seen a kiss like that exchanged between fourteen- and possibly fifteen-year-olds.

He couldn't help thinking that lips as pretty and as

soft-looking as Cass's were being wasted on Ziggy, but the longer the kiss lasted, the less scraggly Ziggy seemed.

When Brad conjured up a vision of himself planting a similar kiss on Cass's lips, it almost knocked the wind out of him.

He remembered Louie's advice: *Get out of this business while you still can.*

But at the moment the best he could do was get out of that department.

So he did.

The shots with the patio furniture made Brad a nervous wreck. He and Cass had to sit on a big blanket surrounded by the plastic ice buckets and picnicware that had been reduced for clearance.

Then he had to push her on a porch swing.

Then he had to sit with her on some stupid wicker love seat so they could toast each other with tall glasses of lemonade.

And Ziggy was watching every minute of it. So were the loyal Baker's shoppers, of course, but it was only Ziggy that bothered him.

After the love-seat shot, Marty said they were going to move on to the clearance active wear; they were to meet in the Sporting-Goods Department in ten minutes.

Ziggy was gone when Brad got there, and Brad wondered if maybe Cass and the Zig Man had gotten busted for making out.

The girl who'd tried to hug him was getting Cass's autograph. When Cass saw Brad, she very casually handed him the girl's book.

"Me?" He looked from Cass to the girl, then back to Cass again.

"Yes, you," said Cass, grinning. "Sign it."

Brad wrote his name on the page next to hers, then handed it back to the girl. But he didn't look at her; he was too busy trying to read Cass's expression. The grin seemed to say, *"You're one of us now. We've bonded."* It also seemed to be telling him that any second now she'd be throwing her arms around him, just as she'd thrown them around Ziggy.

Brad stepped back and gave her a nervous smile. The girl had walked away, giggling.

"That was pretty cool," he admitted.

Cass shrugged. "You'll get used to it." She studied what he was wearing—a pricey tennis outfit that practically screamed "Wimbledon." It matched the flouncy little tennis dress she was wearing. He wondered if he should spin and pose.

"Those look great on you," she told him.

"Thanks."

"You should buy them."

But Brad had seen the price tags. Even with the advertised forty percent off, they were outrageously expensive. He shook his head.

"Why not?" asked Cass. Then her eyes were sparkling and she gave him a big flirty smile. "I'll buy them for you!"

"What?"

Cass was nodding and her golden hair was bobbing. "I have an account here!" she said, touching his sleeve. "I'd love to buy you a great outfit like this."

Brad felt the anger rising. This was more infuriating than Pamela Hartley offering to buy him a soda. But, then, the outfit would be perfect for Jessie's cookout. And Cass was the professional here. If she thought being stormed by a crowd of admirers warranted a present, who was he to argue?

And what thirteen-year-old kid in his right mind would refuse a gift from a potential supermodel?

"Are you sure?" said Brad.

Cass nodded again.

"Well . . . okay. Thanks."

"You're welcome." Cass fluffed her hair. "So I guess you're wondering why *I'm* doing this small-time department-store gig, huh?"

He hadn't been wondering that at all, but he didn't want to be rude. He nodded.

"Well, believe me, it's not because I *want* to. It's just a favor for my father; the owner of the store is his third cousin or something."

"Oh." Brad smiled. "That's pretty generous of you."

"There's nothing generous about it," Cass said matter-of-factly. "They're paying me every penny of my regular fee." She laughed. "I should double it, for having to model clearance."

Then Louie was sticking a tennis racquet in Brad's

hand and Marty was saying, "Swing!" so Brad swung.

He didn't even remember to ask what time it was. He didn't even remember to care.

It was quarter to one when Marty finally said, "Finished!" and Brad realized he was late. A look of panic must have crossed his face because Cass was suddenly very concerned.

"What's wrong?" she asked.

"I'm supposed to be somewhere," Brad said vaguely. "I'm late."

Cass looked up and down the street. "Where's your driver?"

"I don't have a driver," said Brad, and then, because he didn't want to sound unsure of himself, he added, "yet."

Cass was beaming. "I can have mine drop you off!"

"Oh . . . no, thanks . . ." Brad stopped short. Cass's limo was just rounding the corner. He watched in amazement as the long, sleek vehicle pulled up to the curb.

"C'mon," Cass said, taking his arm. "It's not a problem, really."

Brad eyed the limousine. Getting dropped off at Jessie's in this would be an extremely big deal. He felt himself smiling at the thought of it. "Well," he said, "if it's not out of your way, I guess . . ."

"Fabulous," squeaked Cass, and gave his arm a squeeze.

Cass had already squared things with Ms. Heinz about the tennis outfit, so Brad didn't even have to change.

Cass's driver got out to open the car door for them. The guy was roughly the size of a small mountain. He could have been cast in a movie as a hit man for the mob.

Cass beamed at him. "Hi, Terrance."

He tipped his hat. "Hiya, doll. Good shoot?"

"Fabulous."

"Datta girl."

Brad blinked. He thought chauffeurs were supposed to have regal accents and high cheekbones, not Brooklyn accents and biceps the size of bowling balls. He gave Terrance a wary smile. "Hi."

Terrance didn't tip his hat. "Keep yer hands tuh yuhrself back there, Romeo," he growled.

Brad swallowed hard. "Right. Of course."

He hopped into the car after Cass, who was already sipping mineral water out of a tall plastic bottle.

When Terrance was back behind the wheel, he lowered the glass divider that separated the front seat from the enormous backseat, and gave Cass a big smile. "Where to?"

Cass turned to Brad. "Where to?"

Brad told Terrance where Jessie lived. Terrance nodded, then put up the glass divider.

"Is this really your car?" Brad asked, accepting the bottle of water Cass offered.

She nodded. "And Terrance is sort of like a big brother to me."

Brad took a long drink. "A really, *really* big brother."

Cass laughed. "He's been driving me from the start."

"How long ago was that?"

"Thirteen years ago."

Brad's eyes widened. "You started modeling when you were one?"

"One and a half," Cass clarified. "My first job was for a baby-shampoo ad. You know, the kind that doesn't burn your eyes. I had bubbles all over my cheeks. It was a big hit. After that came the detangler ad, then the added-body conditioner. I didn't start doing children's fashions until I was four, and I guess you could say I found my niche." She gave Brad a very grownup smile and handed him a magazine from the seat.

He took it—it was called *Young Miss,* a title he recognized from the magazine section at Zowalski's—and Cass was on the cover.

"Wow. Cool."

"It's my third cover," she told him, and Brad could tell she was excited, even though she was trying to sound careless about the whole thing. "Miranda didn't get a cover till she was fifteen."

"That's great." Brad put the magazine down and finished his water. "I guess you like modeling."

Cass fluttered her eyelashes. "Modeling is my life."

"Baseball's my life," said Brad. "At least, it was."

"Ooooh!" said Cass suddenly, leaning closer to Brad. "I have a totally great idea! How's your schedule?"

"My *schedule?*" Brad shrugged one shoulder. "I don't exactly have one . . ."

"Perfect!" cried Cass. "Because there's this totally happening soiree next Saturday night in the City at Joanna Tandy's." She looked through her eyelashes at Brad. "You know Tandy Models, right? It's only the most totally important modeling agency in Manhattan. My agency. Anyway, Joanna's throwing this totally important bash, and all of us . . . you know, *me,* Zoe March, Tricia Peters, Alicia Franklin, that yummy Gino, and of course Miranda . . . *all* of us are going to be there! You really should come, Brad. It would be terrific exposure for you."

Brad was still trying to figure out what "swaray" meant.

She practically leaped at him. "Say you'll come!" Her arms were around his neck.

"Uh . . . yeah, sure." The driver took an extra-sharp turn into Jessie's street, which sent Brad sliding out of Cass's hug and across the seat.

Brad could see Jessie's house and all the guests' cars parked in the driveway and along the curb. There were people spilling over from the back yard onto the grassy side lawn and everyone seemed to be having a great time.

He leaned forward and rapped on the glass divider. It slid downward.

"It's that blue house," he told Terrance.

"Gotcha'," said Terrance.

"This is where you're going?" said Cass, not even trying to hide her surprise.

"Yeah," said Brad, defensively. "It's a totally important friend's house."

Cass gave him a condescending sniff.

And where does ol' Ziggy live? Brad wanted to say. *The Taj Mahal?* But he didn't. She had given him a ride, after all.

Terrance was pulling up to the curb now, and Brad could see through the car's tinted windows that everyone at the cookout had stopped what they were doing to stare at the big white limousine.

Cass, the professional, knew an audience when she saw one. She rolled down the window and turned her face ever so slightly, just enough to be recognized. In seconds, every girl at the picnic who was old enough to read *Young Miss* came running toward the car.

"It's Cass! Look, it's Cass!"

"I can't believe it!"

"It's really her."

Cass waved out the window.

Brad noticed that even Jessie looked awestruck. Suddenly he couldn't wait to get out of the car. If they were that happy to see Cass, he could only imagine how thrilled they'd be when they saw him!

"Thanks, Cass," he said, opening the door.

"My pleasure. See you Saturday." And she gave him another air kiss in the vicinity of his cheek.

When Brad got out of the car, the girls began giggling. Then Jessie stepped forward. "Hi, Brad."

"Hi, Jess." He gave her one of his grin-snarls.

"I thought maybe you weren't coming."

He shrugged. "The shoot ran late," he said.

"Oh." She seemed to be waiting for something. It didn't occur to Brad that it might be an apology.

Then one of Jessie's cousins was asking him what Cass was like, in real life.

"What's Cass like?" Brad repeated. "She's fabulous! Cass is probably the most fabulous girl I know."

Then he smiled and didn't even notice that Jessie had turned and walked away.

The Brocks' cookout began to break up around five o'clock. All the friends and relatives to whom Brad had been introduced shook his hand and said again what a pleasure it had been to meet him.

Most of the girls seemed reluctant to leave. Personally, Brad was relieved to see them go. He'd spent so much of the afternoon sitting with them, and letting them bring him his second and third cheeseburgers, he hadn't really had much chance to talk to Jessie. In fact, he'd hardly seen her at all.

He didn't have any trouble finding her now, though. The back yard was empty except for himself and Jessie, who was sitting alone on the tire swing that hung from a tall maple near the edge of the property. He walked over to her and leaned against the tree.

"Good cookout," he said. "Your friends and relatives are real nice."

Jessie wrapped her arms around the tire. "You oughta know."

Brad didn't get it. "Uh . . . great cheeseburgers, too." He gave the tire a push and grinned. "Hey, have you ever been in a limo?"

"No."

He gave her another push and tried to think of something that might cheer her up. "I think people were kind of impressed that I showed up with Cass," he said at last.

Jessie dug her sneakers into the dirt and stopped the swing.

"What's wrong?"

"You've changed," said Jessie, slipping out of the tire.

"Yeah?" Brad smiled.

"Yes," said Jessie. "You've really changed." It didn't sound like a compliment.

Brad stuffed his hands in his pockets, confused. "Are you mad at me or something?" He gave the tire swing a little shove with his foot. "Are you mad because I was late?"

"No," said Jessie. "I understand that your shoot ran late. You couldn't help that. But I was sort of upset that you didn't apologize."

"Apologize?" Brad felt as defensive as he had when Cass had sneered at Jessie's house. Funny, he thought, how two girls who were so completely different could give him a feeling that was so completely the same. "I thought showing up in a limo was a pretty good apology."

Jessie's eyes went round. Her cheeks turned red. "Is that what you think, Brad Wilson? You think driving up in some big fancy car makes up for being rude? You think being impressive is more important than being polite?"

Brad shrugged. "Maybe." He realized how arrogant he sounded—but he was already headlong into it. He'd look stupid if he backed off now. "C'mon, Jess . . . you can't tell me that having Cass come to your cookout wasn't kind of cool."

Jessie glared at him. "I didn't want Cass to come to the cookout. I wanted *you* to come to the cookout. But now I wish . . . I wish you just *hadn't*!" There were tears in her eyes when she turned and ran to the house.

Brad watched as the back door slammed behind her. He'd made Jessie cry. The sound of it rang in his ears. She'd cried, and it was his fault. His throat was dry and his head pounded. Had he really acted like such a jerk?

Or . . . had she?

He couldn't help but wonder, as he walked out of the Brocks' yard—had it really been *all* his fault? Okay, so maybe he did owe her an apology for being late, but wasn't she being a little babyish about the limo? Why couldn't she just admit she was as impressed as all the other girls had been? None of them had seemed to care what time it was when he got out of the car.

Brad kicked at a stone in the street. Maybe Jessie was jealous—jealous that he'd been riding in a car with a cover girl. And maybe she'd gotten even more jealous when her friends and cousins couldn't seem to take their eyes off him.

Didn't she realize that the only reason he'd come to the stupid cookout was to be her date? Okay, so he didn't actually spend any time with her, but that *was* the reason he was there. She knew that. So why all the waterworks and door slamming and wishing he hadn't showed?

He kept walking. Jealousy was the only answer. Obviously, Jessie was so crazy about him that she was jealous of Cass and the other girls. Brad allowed a small smile. Heck, it was kind of cute, when he really thought about it. Then he remembered the young movie star's interview he'd read in *GQ*. Hadn't the guy said dating would be difficult?

Brad was finishing up his last overhead lift when his mother knocked. He put down the barbell and said, "Come in."

Mom opened the door and held up the tennis shirt. "Where did this come from?"

"Baker's," he said, beginning his sit-ups.

"Did they give it to you?"

"They didn't," said Brad, curling his chest to his knees. "Cass did."

"*Who* is Cass?"

"The cover model on this month's *Young Miss*."

Brad's mother stepped into the room. "I haven't read *Young Miss* in twenty years, kiddo. Could you be a little more specific?"

Brad stopped crunching. "Cass is a model. She's fourteen and a half, but she looks about twenty. She did the shoot with me today, and she thought the tennis stuff looked good on me, so she bought me the outfit."

"Just like that?"

"Yep." Brad did another sit-up. "I think she likes me."

Mrs. Wilson sat down on the bed. "So is this what fourteen-year-old models do when they like each other? They buy each other clothes?"

"I guess so." Brad stood up, grabbed a dumbbell, and shrugged. "You're askin' the wrong person, Mom. I mean, I'm still new at this."

Mrs. Wilson looked at the tennis shirt she was holding and sighed. "I'm not sure I like the idea of girls buying you expensive things for no reason."

"I told you the reason," said Brad. "She likes me."

"Still . . ."

"Besides, I don't see why you should care, Mom. I mean, if it doesn't bother Ziggy . . ."

"*Ziggy?* Who on earth is Ziggy?"

"Cass's magnificent other."

Mom smiled in spite of herself. "I think you mean significant other?"

"Yeah. Her boyfriend. Ziggy."

"So you're saying this Cass has a boyfriend? And yet she's buying *you* pricey clothes?"

"Yep." Brad switched the weight to his other hand. "And she asked me to a swaray in the City, too."

Mom blinked. "A *soiree*?"

"You're familiar with Joanna Tandy, aren't you?"

Mrs. Wilson planted her hands on her hips. "Not especially."

"Totally important agent," Brad summarized. "Cass thinks I should go and expose myself."

"I bet."

"So can I? I figure we'll be taking the limo, so . . ."

Mom held up her hands to stop him. "I'll think about it. Okay? I will definitely think about it, and we'll see."

Brad knew better than to push a "we'll see." He huffed out a few more bicep curls as his mother watched, shaking her head and looking very confused.

"By the way," she asked at last, "how was the cookout?"

"Okay."

"That's it . . . just okay?"

Brad put down the dumbbell and checked his biceps in the mirror. "All the girls wanted to sit with me, and then Jessie got jealous and cried, but other than that, it was just your basic cookout."

"Just your *basic* cookout . . . and a *soiree* in New York City." Mom tossed the shirt over her shoulder. "You know something? I think I liked it better when you used to come home rambling about curveballs and batting averages."

CHAPTER NINE

Bottom of the Ninth
. . . Bases Loaded

Jill was a basket case!

It was Friday night. T.J. had finally gotten up the nerve to ask her out. Brad and Meggie sat on the couch, watching, as Jill scurried from room to room—rolling her hair, doing her nails, unrolling her hair, changing her clothes, screaming for Nana to help find the right purse.

It was all very entertaining.

"Does this look all right?" Jill asked, stopping in the middle of the family room to run yet another outfit by them. "What do you think?"

"Fine," said Meggie.

"Nice," said Brad.

"Lovely," said Mrs. Wilson.

Jill went back to her room to change. "What time

is it?" came her panicked voice from the bedroom.

"Five minutes later than the last time you asked," called Nana, rolling her eyes. "And I don't suppose we have any hope of the man being late. He only lives across the driveway."

"Where's the styling mousse?" Jill cried from her room. "I can't find the mousse!" She dashed back into the family room and gave Brad's mom a desperate look. "Do you have the mousse?"

Mrs. Wilson shook her head.

Jill turned to Nana. "Ma? Did you use the mousse today?"

"No, dear."

"Meggie, honey, were you playing with my mousse by any chance?"

Meggie swore she wasn't.

They hadn't noticed Brad leaving the room, or returning with the narrow can of styling foam. He cleared his throat. The women looked at him.

"Uh . . . I had it," he said. "In my room."

Jill lunged for the can and disappeared in a blur toward the bathroom.

"I was trying out a new look," he said, his voice husky with embarrassment. "I thought my hair needed some volume."

Meggie cocked an eyebrow. "You wanted to make your hair louder?"

"No, stupid, not louder. Fuller, fluffier. More oomphy."

Nana patted his hair. "Ya' know, I thought you looked

a little taller. I'd say you oomphed yourself at least three inches."

His mother bit her lip. "How much mousse did you use?"

"Uh . . ."

"The whole can!" came Jill's shout from the bathroom. "He used the *whole* can!" She stomped into the family room and glared at her nephew. "Thanks a lot, Bradley. Now I've got to go on this date with oomphless hair!"

Brad shoved his hands in his pockets. "Sorry."

The doorbell spared Brad from further reprimand. "I'll get it!" He opened the door to a very nervous T.J. "Hi."

"Hi." T.J. swallowed hard.

"C'mon in." Brad led his friend to the family room, which was now empty. This, he knew, was part of that girls-against-the-boys game: the girl was never supposed to be ready on time, or else she'd seem too eager.

"She's not ready?" asked T.J., wiping his palms on his pants legs and looking panicked.

"She's ready," Brad assured him. "She just doesn't want you to know she's ready."

"Oh. Okay." T.J. was looking at Brad's hair with a strange expression.

"So . . ." said Brad, taking a seat on the sofa. "Where are you taking her?"

"Uh . . . well . . . dinner." T.J. sat down beside Brad. "I thought we'd go out for dinner."

Brad gave him a nod. "Just don't go to a fast-food joint," he advised. "She hates the salads."

T.J. laughed in spite of himself. "No, I was thinking more along the lines of Chez Vincent's. Somewhere where we can order appetizers I can't pronounce and champagne I can't afford."

"Sounds great," said Jill, appearing in the doorway with Nana, Meggie, and Brad's mom on her heels. "I love champagne."

"Oh." T.J. sprung up from the sofa. "Hi."

"Sorry to keep you waiting . . ." said Jill. Brad rolled his eyes.

"What's champagne?" asked Meggie.

"It's wine," said Nana, "that's in a really good mood."

T.J. laughed. It was a nervous laugh.

Then Jill was saying, "Shall we?" and T.J. opened the front door for her.

"You kids have fun," Brad teased. "And don't be too late."

"Enjoy yourselves," said Mrs. Wilson.

"Don't do anything I wouldn't do . . ." said Nana, chuckling.

Meggie was too dreamy-eyed to say anything.

When the door closed behind them, Brad put his feet up on the coffee table and smiled. Tomorrow night, he'd be heading out that same door on his way to a totally important soiree in Manhattan—but there'd be no sweaty palms for him. He was just wondering whether he should make Cass think he wasn't ready, when Mom sat down beside him.

Automatically, she brushed his feet from the table. "Let's talk."

"About what?"

"About tomorrow night. About this party in the City."

"Zoe March is going to be there."

"Is Zoe March the one who does those perfume commercials?" asked Meggie. "The ones with all the blue fire in the background, and the whispery conversation that doesn't make any sense?"

Brad nodded. "And Alicia Franklin, and Tricia Peters."

"The skinny ones," said Meggie. "With the sad eyes."

"I was hoping for a little more than just the guest list," said Mom. "For instance, who's chaperoning? Is there going to be alcohol served?"

"I dunno." Brad shrugged. "What difference does it make? I'm not old enough to drink."

"*That's* what difference it makes," said Nana. "These kids live in a different world, Brad. My guess is, they're pretty sophisticated."

Brad remembered the way Cass and Ziggy had been kissing, but didn't mention it. "Don't you trust me?"

"Of course I trust you, honey." Mom touched his hair. It sort of sprung back at her. "This is just happening so fast, and you're very young . . ."

"I can handle it, Mom." Brad gave her a confident smile. "It's just a party."

"You'd better not smoke!" said Meggie. "Smoking rots your lungs and turns your fingers yellow."

"I'm not gonna smoke, Meg. I'm an athlete, remember?" He picked up the remote and turned on the television, hoping this would end the conversation.

"Athlete or no athlete," Mom said, standing, "you will not leave this house until I have the address and phone number where you're going to be. Clear?"

Brad sighed. "Crystal."

When the females left the room, he put his feet back on the table. At least he had the answer to his question about pretending not to be ready.

He'd be on time, all right—he might even be early. When Cass arrived, Brad was going to get out of the house as fast as possible.

And he didn't care how eager it made him seem.

Brad looked good in black.

His shirt was black, his jeans were black, his belt was black, and the heavy-soled boots he'd bought that morning were black as well.

"Who died?" asked Meggie from the doorway.

"Shut up." Brad was studying himself in the mirror. "It's called fashion."

Meggie wrinkled her nose. "It's called black."

He ignored her and picked up the money his mother had left for him on the dresser. He was stuffing it into his pocket when the doorbell rang.

"Cass!" screamed Meggie and bolted for the front door.

But it wasn't Cass—it was Terrance. Meggie gave a little yelp and took a step back.

"Cass is already in da' City," the driver explained. "She had a shoot there this afternoon."

"Bummer," said Meggie.

"Yeah," said Terrance.

A look from Mom reminded Brad to have Terrance write down Joanna Tandy's address and phone number. Terrance complied, but Brad thought he heard the big guy snickering as he wrote.

When Brad said goodbye to his family, Mom's "Have fun" sounded like a cross between a wish and a warning. He followed Terrance to the car, then waved from the backseat.

And he was off.

When they turned the corner of Brad's street, Terrance rolled down the glass divider.

"Want somethin' ta' drink?"

"Uh . . . sure." Brad leaned forward. "There's a McDonald's near the highway—I guess we could hit the drive-thru . . ."

"There's a bar back there."

"Bar?" Brad's eyes roamed the leathery cocoon that was the backseat of Cass's limo. He remembered the icy-cold bottle of water he'd had the day Cass had given him a ride to Jessie's. He'd assumed she'd brought it along in a cooler. He hadn't known there was an actual bar on board. Terrance must have noticed him searching in the rearview.

"Whaddya blind, kid? Right there. Near the television."

"Oh." Moments later, Brad was guzzling a mineral water and feeling a little less intimidated by the appliance-sized chauffeur. After all, the guy had offered him a drink. He decided to take a shot at conversation.

"So, Terrance . . ." he began, leaning forward again. "Hey, do you like people to call you Terrance or Terry?"

The chauffeur hit the turn signal. "Depends on da' people."

That remark was followed by the whir of the divider going up.

Then Brad remembered that in movies the rich people riding in limousines rarely spoke to their drivers. Maybe Terrance was just following the rules. So Brad sat back in his seat and decided to enjoy the rest of the ride.

Fat chance.

Riding in the back alone, cut off from Terrance—correction, *the driver*—by a big old hunk of glass, was nerve-racking. It was creepy.

But evidently this was the way it was done.

So Brad sat back and did it.

Brad was fiddling with the buttons on the cell phone when he heard the whir of the divider going down.

"Watch it, hotshot," came Terrance's voice over the seat. "I don't wan'cha accidentally callin' Tahiti on dat thing."

"Sorry."

The driver gave a little jerk of his head, motioning toward Brad's window. "Feast yer eyes, kid. I get the feeling you don't get down to the Big Apple much."

Brad put the phone down and turned to the window. His mouth nearly fell open at what he saw. Across the river, the Manhattan skyline pulsed with what had to be a million lights. The buildings reached into the blue-purple dusk like rows of enormous stone-and-steel trophies. Brad gaped at it. The proud, angular, jagged skyline was like a three-dimensional geometry lesson.

Soon they were entering the City itself. More lights! Lights from cars and signs and buildings. And it seemed that almost everything that gave off light gave off noise as well. Brad could hear it through the closed window, the beeping and blaring and singing and shouting. It was loud. It was maddening.

It was beautiful!

Terrance hit a switch in the front seat and Brad's window slid down to let the noise and the light in. It was even louder now, brighter, more exciting—electrified, supercharged.

This was the City. This was *New . . . York . . . City*!

He stuck his head out the window and let the sounds assail him. Car horns, and music spilling out from the bars, and people everywhere.

The limo glided through the roar, and the light rained down on him.

Somewhere in this miraculous place, Joanna Tandy's miraculous party was going on. And minutes from now, Brad would arrive in this miraculous limousine to be part of it.

It was like hitting a grand slam.

No—it was better.

"Somebody *lives* here?"

Cass took his arm, giggling. "Of course. Joanna lives here."

"Man!"

They were waiting for an elevator in the marble lobby of the most elegant building Brad had ever seen, and Cass seemed more bubbly than ever. When the elevator doors opened, she stepped toward them. Brad felt her wobble.

"You okay?"

Her answer was a very goofy giggle. The elevator lurched upward, then glided smoothly to the top floor of the building. When the doors slid open, Brad found himself in a miniature version of the downstairs lobby—gleaming light fixtures, cool pink marble, and expensive paintings. At one end was a pair of double doors. He could hear the party through them.

"Here we are," cooed Cass, dragging him toward the doors and pushing them open. The smell of cigarette smoke hit them hard.

Brad had never seen so many people in one place in his life—and every one of them seemed to be more beautiful than the next. There were stuffy-looking men in suits and silk ties, and there were tall, intense-looking women in sparkling gowns.

"The agents," Cass explained with a knowing air.

She shouldered past them, toward a small knot of teenagers at the far end of the room. Brad followed her, noticing that many of the agents paused in their gossiping and drinking to look at him with interest.

"He's new," one of them said.

"Mouthwatering, isn't he?" drawled another.

When they reached the teenage crowd, Cass squealed, "Tricia! When did you get here? Great shoes!"

Tricia shrugged, and her eyes locked on Brad.

"Hi," he said. "I'm Brad."

"Uh-huh."

He wasn't sure what to say to that one.

Tricia was handing Cass a cigarette, which, to Brad's surprise, Cass accepted. A skinny girl with heavy eye makeup appeared and gave Cass a hug. She was at least six inches taller than Brad.

"Saw your little cover," she said to Cass. "Nice."

"Thanks," said Cass, lighting the cigarette. "Having fun?"

"A drag," said the girl. She held out her hand for Brad to shake. "Alicia."

"Brad."

"Hello, *you*!" came a girl's voice from the knot. She

was pushing her way toward them. She had icy-blond hair and earrings that looked like medieval torture devices. She also had big gray eyes and perfect teeth. Brad felt a weird stab through his chest—his heart was either speeding up or stopping, he couldn't tell which—and suddenly his mouth went dry. This girl was . . . well, the only word for her was gorgeous! He didn't even notice Zoe and Alicia scurry away.

"Miranda!" Cass flung her arms around the gray-eyed girl, and Brad noticed some ashes from her cigarette landing in Miranda's hair, but he wasn't sure it was accidental. "How was Paris?"

"Oh, we had some fun. But Laurence was up to his usual head games. You know." A waiter appeared, holding a tray of slender, delicate-looking glasses filled with a bubbly, golden drink. Miranda plucked one and handed it to Cass; the next one she gave to Brad.

"Know what champagne is?" he asked the girls. "It's wine . . . in a really good mood."

Miranda studied him with her stormy eyes for a long moment before turning back to Cass. "Where did you find him?"

Before Cass could answer, her manager appeared at her elbow and whisked her away to meet some photographer, leaving Brad more or less alone with Miranda.

"Come with me," she ordered. "Let's mingle."

What else could he do? He mingled.

Actually, it felt less like mingling and more like being dragged around the room behind Miranda, holding a champagne glass. He'd sworn to his mom that he wouldn't dare drink, but at one point Miranda stopped to chat with a girl who was wearing an extremely short, extremely tight dress. Brad was so mesmerized that he accidentally took a sip of champagne. It wasn't bad. It made the roof of his mouth tingle and the inside of his cheeks itch, but he kind of liked it. Then Tight-Dress excused herself and went slinking through the crowd.

"Poor thing," Miranda told Brad in a whisper. "That dress is a colossal mistake."

Brad didn't understand that one. It looked fine to him. He took another sip of champagne, and while they went on mingling, his mouth went on tingling.

They killed some time watching a video of some recent fashion show on Joanna's big-screen TV. Brad thought the runway models walked as if they were part panther.

They joined a group of agents discussing Armani, which Brad figured was some little Third World country he'd never heard of. "Let's get an opinion from the younger set," one said, looking at Brad.

He answered with a bluff. "I think the President should keep U.S. military assistance there to a minimum."

Bad bluff.

"Get real," said Miranda. "Do you really not know who Armani is?"

Brad shook his head, feeling like an idiot.

"He's a designer, not a foreign country."

Brad took a fast drink of champagne. "In that case, I think the President should send in as many troops as possible."

That got the people laughing. Some actually agreed with Brad, while others said they'd enlist on Armani's side.

"War as a metaphor for fashion," crooned one of the nearby agents. "How true!"

Brad's error had turned into a home run.

Miranda gave the agent a glowing smile, which she kept locked in place when she turned, tugging Brad with her. At first, he assumed the smile meant she no longer thought he was an idiot.

"Brad, honey," she said through her teeth. "You're adorable and a stranger in these parts, so I'm going to give you a second chance." Then she turned up the wattage on her smile and waved to a reed-thin woman across the room, before turning her attention back to Brad. "Speak less and smile more. And don't upstage me again."

After that, Brad was introduced to three rock stars, an up-and-coming screenwriter, a woman Miranda called the hottest P.R. rep in the galaxy, whatever that meant, and a former talk-show host.

He also drank two more glasses of champagne and started to feel fuzzy.

"Hey," he said. "Hey, I know that guy!" Brad pointed across the room, splashing a little champagne out of his glass. It was the *pour l'homme* guy he'd seen in *GQ;* he was wearing jeans and a snug-fitting T-shirt and drinking beer out of a bottle.

"You know Gino?" said Miranda.

"Well, no, I don't *know* him. I've just seen him in a magazine."

Miranda rolled her eyes. "Come on, country boy. I'll introduce you."

The next thing Brad knew, he was watching Miranda smoosh herself against Gino. It was a full-body block that was supposed to pass for a handshake. She was still wrapped around him when she said, "Gino, Brad. Brad, Gino."

"Hey," said Brad.

Gino nodded. He held Miranda a little longer, then released her with a nibbly kiss on her neck. As they walked away, Brad saw some guy in a dark suit come over and smoosh *himself* up against Gino.

"Is he your boyfriend?" Brad asked Miranda, downing the last of his champagne.

"Gino?" Miranda narrowed her eyes and gave a wicked little laugh. "Gino is *everybody's* boyfriend."

Brad didn't think he *wanted* to understand that one. The champagne was hot in his stomach and his eyes were burning. "I'm starving," he said.

"So am I," came a voice from behind him. He whirled, to see Cass standing there.

"Hello, you," he said, and felt instantly stupid.

Cass didn't seem to notice. She was tugging him toward a well-stocked buffet table which held enormous platters of exotic-looking food.

For some reason, Brad found himself remembering

the paper plates, cheeseburgers, and potato salad from Jessie's cookout. Nothing here looked or smelled familiar, but Brad took a china plate and began filling it.

Cass studied the table. "I hate sushi."

Brad figured Sushi was probably a friend of Armani's. "Me, too."

He watched Cass put three slices of kiwi and some tofu on her plate.

"I thought you were starving," he said.

"I am!"

That's when he began to notice what the people around him were eating—or, more accurately, *not* eating. The models put next to nothing on their plates and then stood around holding them as if they didn't know what the food was for.

When Cass asked if he'd like more champagne, the mere mention of the word made his head hurt.

"What time is it?" he asked.

"Early," she answered casually. "Only two."

"In the morning?" Brad's eyes flew open. "Two o'clock *in the morning?*"

"Problem?"

"Big problem! I was supposed to be home at . . ." He closed his eyes. "Well, technically, *yesterday.*"

Cass found this hilarious. She laughed. Brad didn't. At that moment, he wanted to slug her. His vision was so cloudy from the champagne, chances were he would have missed.

What he didn't miss was the tall, red-haired woman in the silver dress making her way toward them.

"That's Joanna!" said Cass breathlessly, gripping his arm. "Let me introduce you."

Brad forced himself to stand up straight. The totally important agent-slash-hostess was smiling at him.

"Hello," she said in a buttery voice. "Are you, by any chance, Brad Wilson?"

Cass's long nails dug into his skin, reminding him to answer.

"Yes, I am," said Brad, trying to shake off Cass's grip. *She's going to offer me a contract,* he told himself—and the last thing he wanted was to accept the offer with Cass clawing him.

"Oh . . . well, Brad . . ." Joanna extended her arm, holding something out to him. "This is for you."

A contract? A million bucks? He was finding it difficult to concentrate, between the champagne and Cass's clinging. It took him a moment to realize that what Joanna was handing him was a cordless phone.

"It's . . . your mother," the agent said stiffly.

Suddenly Cass wasn't clinging anymore.

The ride out of Manhattan was vastly different from the ride in, especially to a nauseated kid riding by himself in the back of a limo.

This trip, Brad didn't even notice the lights, and the only noise he was aware of was a sickly sloshing sound from his stomach . . . that and the sound of Terrance laughing at him.

He rode the last twenty minutes with his head between his knees, trying to still the churning in his guts, and thinking.

Thinking how what had begun as the best night of his life wound up being the most humiliating.

His mother had called the party at two o'clock. It had taken a while for Cass to connect with Terrance, since she'd told him not to come back for her until three. Then there was the hour's drive home from the City.

So it was after 4 A.M. when Brad's feet hit the cracked pavement of his driveway. When Terrance saw that Mrs. Wilson was waiting in the doorway, he laughed harder than ever.

Brad slammed the car door behind him and stormed up the walk to the house. His mother flung open the screen door and held it. Brad practically flew past her and into the house. It was hard to tell which of them looked angrier.

"I can't believe you *called*!" he growled.

"I can't believe you *didn't* call," Mom growled back. "You were supposed to be home at eleven!"

"Come *on*!" Brad threw up his hands. "Some of the people didn't even show up until eleven!"

"Well, I'm not *their* mother. I'm *your* mother." She gave him a fiery look. "And I told you to be home at eleven."

"I lost track of time."

"I'll say you did!" Mrs. Wilson dragged her hand through her hair, and for a split second her relief seemed to outweigh her rage. "Do you have any idea how frightened I was?" she asked softly. "I couldn't imagine what happened . . ."

"I was having fun, that's what happened!"

"Well, you should have called. I'm sure there was a cell phone at every punch bowl!"

Brad rolled his eyes. "I wasn't drinking punch, I was drinking cham . . ." *Uh-oh.*

"Go on." Mom folded her arms, tapping her foot. "You were drinking *cham* . . . Cham *what,* Brad? Sham—*poo?* I don't think so."

Brad looked down at his boots and shrugged. "I had a sip," he muttered. If he hadn't been swaying, she might have believed him.

"So you were drinking champagne?"

"Everybody was drinking it!" Brad snapped his head up to give her a smart-aleck look. "And don't bother with that stupid George Washington Bridge thing, okay?"

Mom steadied herself with a long, slow breath. "Grounded," she said through clenched teeth. "Indefinitely."

"Are you *serious*?" Brad was shouting now. "This *sucks!*"

In a flash, his mother was standing so close that her

nose touched his. She was clutching his chin tight between her fingers, and her voice was pure heat.

"You listen to me, young man. They can name you model-of-the-year for all I care, but you will *not* raise your voice to me like that *ever* again! Do you understand? I was your mother long before they put your face on that billboard, mister." She let go of his chin as quickly as she'd grabbed it. There were tears in her eyes.

For a moment, they stood there, looking at each other.

Then he was moving—stepping back, turning toward the door. The next thing he knew, he was heading down the walk and into the street.

Brad ran.

He ran all the way to the ball field.

He jumped the curb, crossed the damp grass, and when he reached home plate, he ran faster—faster, down the first-base line, his boots pounding the dirt until he hit the bag, where he lowered his left shoulder and steered himself, steaming, toward second—faster.

His arms pumped, his chest heaved. He was sweating at second, dripping wet at third, and still he ran, rounding third base and pouring it all into the small, straight sprint to the plate, where his boots made a hollow thump against the rubber. It was not the fast, familiar scratch, the metallic scrape his spikes used to make. This sound was dull, like a punch in the gut.

This sound hurt.

And his head hurt, and his eyes, and his leg muscles hurt, too. No, his leg muscles *killed.* The champagne was sour in his stomach now, and the pleasant itch in his cheeks had gone sticky.

Brad bent over and threw up in the batter's box.

T.J. was leaning over him when Brad opened his eyes. "Hey, buddy. You okay?"

Brad blinked. He was curled into a little ball on the bench of the dugout. "Teej?" He sat up slowly. The sky across the field was pale gray. "Yeah. I'm okay, I guess. What time is it?"

"Five-thirty."

"Man . . ."

"Your mom sent me to find you," T.J. explained. "She's scared to death!" It was the first time Brad ever heard T.J. sound fatherly. Not good fatherly—but ferociously fatherly.

"I don't blame her," Brad said softly, lowering his eyes.

"She said you were drinking." When Brad didn't deny it, T.J. sat down on the bench and let his breath out in a long rush. "I feel sorta responsible for that."

"You weren't even there."

"Yeah, but the other night I was talking about ordering champagne and . . . I don't know, I was afraid maybe I gave you the idea. Maybe you thought if I was drinking, it was okay for you to . . ."

"No," said Brad quickly. "It wasn't your fault. It was mine." Brad rubbed his forehead. "Mine and Miranda's."

"Miranda? You were drinking champagne with Miranda, from the swimsuit calendars?" A fast flicker of admiration crossed T.J.'s face. Then he shook his head hard. "I suppose I could see how you got carried away, but still, Brad . . . I thought you were smarter than that."

"So did I."

In the silence that passed between them, Brad became aware of the noise.

It was a noise he remembered. He'd heard it the morning he'd sat on the mound to watch his billboard go up. It was the sound of men climbing scaffolding beyond the outfield fence.

Brad watched, eyes wide, as his billboard face slowly, systematically began to disappear—to vanish behind the layers of another Baker's ad. One minute it was there and the next . . .

"So much for the big push in young men's casual," murmured T.J., placing a hand on Brad's shoulder.

Brad gaped. It had truly never occurred to him that the billboard would change, and only now did he realize how ridiculous that was. Ridiculous and naïve, egotistical and stupid.

"Let's go," he said, getting up from the bench.

In the time it took to reach T.J.'s car, the whole left side of Brad's face had been covered up. Brad got in the car, and he didn't look back.

He couldn't.

CHAPTER TEN

Extra Innings

There is nothing like a house full of angry women. It seemed that, in the wake of last night's trauma, the only thing his mother, his aunt, and his grandmother could bring themselves to do was clean.

They cleaned everything—every floor, every closet, every tabletop. The lemony scent of furniture polish permeated the place, and the wood floors had been pastewaxed within an inch of their lives. Walking across the family-room floor was now a treacherous task.

Brad tried to sleep, but the banging of broom handles and the smell of ammonia made it impossible. He considered offering his help (he'd been known to scrub a mean toilet in his day, and he was a pro with a vacuum cleaner), but decided against it.

So at noon Sunday he was sitting at the kitchen table

eating cold cereal and watching as Jill reorganized the contents of the pantry.

He hesitated a moment before he spoke. "Did you and T.J. have fun on your date?"

"Yes," was the curt response.

"Was he scared?"

"Only at first." Jill slammed a box of rice onto a shelf.

Brad attempted a smile. "That's great. Is he your significant other now?"

"If you mean is he my boyfriend—yes, I guess so." Jill turned and gave him a look. "But please . . . spare me your significant-other crap, okay?"

Brad leaned back in his chair, surprised and hurt. "I was just trying to . . ."

"To what?" Jill folded her arms across her chest. "To impress me?"

"To make conversation."

"Well, you don't sound like the Bradley I know." Jill sighed. "What's happened to you? One day you're the sweetest kid on earth, losing sleep over an unreliable curveball—and the next, you're staying out all night drinking champagne."

"And calling Bernie fatso," added Meggie, slipping in from the well-waxed family room. "His sister told me you made him feel so bad that he didn't eat anything but celery for two days."

Jill gave her nephew an I-told-you-so raise of her eyebrows.

"I didn't mean it that way," said Brad, pushing his ce-

194

real bowl aside. "And why didn't Bernie just tell me to get lost? We're friends—he could have told me to mind my own business."

"Maybe he was afraid to insult the famous Billboard Boy," snapped Meggie. She shook her head. "Poor Bernie."

Brad closed his eyes and remembered the day Bernie Klemp had called the game, just to keep him from being humiliated. "What else did Bernie's sister say?"

"She said everybody was sick of you, and now that your big dumb face is off the billboard, the kids aren't going to put up with you and your monster ego anymore."

"Easy, Meg," said Jill, softening. "I wouldn't say your brother is exactly a monster."

"Yes he is!" said Meggie. "He's been telling the guys how to wear their hair, making fun of Norman's clothes . . . Even Jessie Brock said . . ."

Brad felt his chest lighten. "What? What did Jessie say?"

"She said you'd changed, Brad. That's what she said."

Glumly, Brad went to his room to get dressed. He didn't have to pull the shade, because for some reason today there were no girls looking in his window. He wondered why he wasn't more relieved about it than he was.

And then it hit him.

Brad was on the phone in seconds flat, dialing Ms. Heinz's number. Even though it was a Sunday, he hoped she'd be at work, since the store was open.

"Public relations . . ." she said when she answered.

"Hi, Ms. Heinz. This is Brad Wilson."

She hesitated a moment. He was afraid she'd forgotten him already. "How may I help you, Bradley?"

"Well, I was just wondering . . . uh, if the next billboard . . . if I could, sorta, maybe . . ." He cleared his throat. "I was thinking one of the formal-wear shots might make a good billboard."

"The tuxedo shots were fabulous," said Ms. Heinz, and Brad's heart leaped. "But . . ."

"But what? Can't you use me on the next billboard?"

Ms. Heinz was laughing now. "Considering our next big push is going to be in ladies' nightgowns and foundation garments, darling, I doubt it very much."

"Oh." Brad gripped the phone. "Right. I guess not."

"Cheer up, Brad," said Ms. Heinz. "You've got a fabulous future in this business, believe me. You've just got to be patient. Now, you're—what? Thirteen? Fourteen? You've got at least two good years left in you. Maybe more, if you want to get an agent, give the runways a try, go international . . . Remember, you've got the Look."

How could he forget?

"Do you think you'll have anything else for me?" he asked. "Do you think you'll be able to, ya' know . . . use me?"

"Use you?" Ms. Heinz gave a steely chuckle that made Brad wish he could rephrase that last part. "Well, of course, Bradley. Cass ate up a lot of our budget—her price just skyrocketed after that *Young Miss* cover. So naturally, for our spring promos, we'll have to use some-one with a reasonable fee schedule. Like you."

"Yeah," Brad grumbled. "Reasonable."

Brad hung up the phone, allowing everything to sink in—in all honesty, given the last twenty-four hours, he really didn't care if he ever modeled again. He missed his friends, he missed Jessie, and he missed standing over the plate wondering whether he was going to hit a miraculous line drive or ground out to short. He never would have believed he could miss grounding out to short, but he did.

But what was sinking in now was the realization that if he never modeled again, Ms. Heinz could easily find some other bush leaguer to—what had she said?—use.

He lowered himself into the chair beside the phone and immediately popped up again. He'd sat down on something—his *GQ* magazine. He lifted it from the seat cushion, then slumped back into the chair and fanned the pages, the slick, glossy-smooth pages featuring those party-type people in all manner of high-concept pho-tographs, from bright color to muted black-and-white.

They were quite a contrast to the billboard over center field for which he had been paid only a reasonable fee.

A weird tingle of embarrassment filled him. One crummy billboard in a small town, versus international ex-posure in a highly respected fashion magazine. How could he ever have presumed to put himself up against the Ginos and Mirandas or even the Casses of the world? It was the same as trying to outpitch Nolan Ryan, or outhit Willie Mays. It was . . . well, *stupid*! Impossible, and stupid.

Sure, he had ridden in their limos, drunk their classy drinks, and tried to speak their Fabulous-Hello-You language, but he knew now that he hadn't really been part of it. He'd been an onlooker, the new flavor—and for all he knew, they'd laughed at him through all of it.

Brad sank lower in the chair, wishing he could hide from himself. Suddenly modeling seemed to *belong* to Gino and Miranda. If the modeling world were a stadium, then Gino and Miranda had box seats behind the third-base dugout, and Brad's view was from the cheap seats.

But it had always been fun in the bleachers. He remembered the afternoons when he and his father would head down to the Bronx to watch the Yanks play. They'd feast on hot dogs and peanuts, and sing along with other bleacher creatures during the seventh-inning stretch.

He'd wondered what the game looked like from the box seats.

His dad had told him, "Not this good."

Brad slapped through a fashion spread that featured a few executive types and a Gino look-alike. The backgrounds suggested Paris, Milan.

Brad's big shoot had taken place in an industrial park a few blocks from his own home.

So he'd made the billboard—nearly the only billboard in town. In the world of modeling, how big of a deal could it be to be a big deal in a town that only has a few billboards? So some dippy girls had knocked on his window. Maybe that was just because, in Haverton, there weren't any other windows to knock on. So one up-and-coming supermodel had bought him a tennis outfit. That didn't exactly make him a star. It had made him *think* he was a star, but what did that make him?

A dope.

The tingle of embarrassment was now an actual ache. Brad dropped the magazine on the freshly polished coffee table and sighed.

He was so lost in his thoughts that at first he didn't notice Meggie standing beside him.

"You okay?"

"Sure, I'm fine. For a monster."

"I didn't really mean that." Meggie gave him an apologetic smile.

A *beautifully* apologetic smile—it gave him an idea.

"Come with me!" he said, taking her arm.

"You can't go out! You're grounded."

"They're so busy cleaning they won't even know I'm gone. Come on, Meg. This is urgent."

She looked at him hard. "Where are we going?"

He told her. Then he had to chase her around the entire house, catch her, and drag her along with him as he snuck out the door.

It wasn't easy. But he knew it was going to be worth it.

Brad knocked on the door to Ms. Heinz's office with one hand. He was struggling to keep hold of Meggie with the other.

"Come in."

He opened the door and shoved Meggie in ahead of him.

"Why, hello, Bradley." Ms. Heinz seemed surprised, maybe even a little annoyed, to see him.

"Hi, Ms. Heinz. How's it goin'?"

"Fine, thank you." The public-relations lady strummed her fingers impatiently on her desk, watching as Brad forcibly lowered his wriggling sister into a chair. "May I ask what brings you here? I thought I'd explained on the phone . . ."

"Well," said Brad, keeping a strong hand on Meggie's shoulder, "I've been thinking about my modeling career . . ."

"Hmmmm." Ms. Heinz was looking down her nose at him.

"See, last night, I was talking with Miranda . . ."

Ms. Heinz's eyes flew open. "Miranda?"

"Yeah." Brad nodded, being careful not to let Meggie escape. "Anyway, Miranda said sometimes the biggest mistake a model can make is overexposure. And I figure, being on one of the only billboards in town, I was big-time overexposed. That's why I've decided to take a little break from modeling. I mean, Look or no Look—Haverton's probably sick of looking at me."

Ms. Heinz blinked. "Well . . . perhaps . . ."

"But Meggie," said Brad quickly, "Meggie is as under-exposed as you can get. And everybody I know says she's the cutest little kid they've ever seen."

"She does look a lot like you . . ." Ms. Heinz admitted.

"Right," said Brad. "Meg's got great hair, perfect teeth . . . and she's smart! Joanna Tandy says . . ."

"Joanna Tandy?! You *know* Joanna Tandy?"

"Sure." Brad gave an offhanded shrug. "Used her phone." He knew he was exaggerating his relationship to the renowned agent, but he liked seeing Ms. Heinz squirm. "Anyway, Joanna believes that a model's most important quality is intelligence. Meggie's practically a genius."

Hearing her brother's praise made Meggie stop wriggling. She gave Ms. Heinz one of her biggest smiles.

"Meggie can do for Girls 7 to 14," Brad explained, "what I did for Young Men's Casual! And she's only seven, so she can do it longer!"

Ms. Heinz was studying Meggie carefully. "She is precious," she said thoughtfully.

"Precious . . . and reasonable," said Brad, but he doubted very much if Ms. Heinz caught the sarcasm.

"You know, we *are* planning a huge promotion in girls' separates for Columbus Day, and she *would* be perfectly fetching in plaid, wouldn't she?"

Brad and Meggie exchanged glances, but Ms. Heinz hardly noticed.

"And we could definitely use her for the pre-Christmas toy-sale spectacular! I can see her now . . . kneeling beside the Baby Betsy Dream Cradle . . ."

"And don't forget electronics," said Meggie, batting her big green eyes. "I kick butt at computer games!"

"Fabulous!"

When Brad and Meggie left the public-relations office, Meggie was holding a scrap of notepaper with her hourly rate written on it.

"It'll be fun, Meg," Brad assured her as they stepped into the elevator.

"But I thought you wanted to be the one earning a paycheck," said Meggie, pushing the button for the first floor. "I thought you wanted to be the man of the house."

"I did," Brad admitted. "But I figure I've got time. I'm just gonna be the boy of the house for now. You can bring home the bacon."

Meggie laughed. Then her face became serious. "You really were terrific on the billboard," she said, stepping out of the elevator. "But you're a lot more terrific off it."

Brad couldn't have agreed with her more.

Brad managed to sneak Meggie back into the house unnoticed, but he still had one more place to go. When he told his sister why he had to sneak out again, she promised not to rat on him.

"Where do you think you're going?" Nana asked when Brad skidded across the family room toward the front door. "You happen to be grounded."

"I know. But, Nana, this is an emergency." Brad's eyes were pleading. "I've been a jerk—to everybody—and I really need to apologize to Jessie."

Nana put down the feather duster she was holding. "Go ahead. Your mother's scrubbing the grout in the bathtub. She'll be in there at least another hour. She probably won't even know you're missing."

Brad almost laughed. He'd gone all the way to Baker's, gotten Meggie a job, and had returned, all without being caught. He was just congratulating himself on having put one over on Nana when she whacked him playfully on the head with her duster.

". . . Again!"

His mouth dropped open. "You knew I was gone?"

Nana rolled her eyes. "Give me a little credit, will you? I raised one son, and one spitfire of a daughter. *Nobody* sneaks out without me knowing about it!"

"Why didn't you tell Mom? Why didn't you stop me?"

"Well, I decided it must have been something important if you were willing to risk getting into more trouble." She winked at him. "In spite of the way you've been acting lately, I know you're basically a good kid."

Brad gave her a smile. "So you don't think Mom'll miss me?"

"If she does," said Nana with a sigh, "I'll cover for you. As long as it means getting the old Brad back."

Brad felt a stab of guilt. "I really changed, didn't I?"

"Yes. But it didn't last long. Besides, I knew you'd come around eventually."

"How did you know?"

"Well, for starters," said Nana, touching his cheek, "you never lost your father's smile."

"Good," said Brad. "Because I think I'm gonna need it."

He found Jessie in her back yard on the tire swing.

And Skeff was pushing her.

"Look," sneered Skeff, "it's Mr. Billboard." He halted the swing, placing his hand on Jessie's shoulder as if he owned her. Brad was glad when she gently shrugged it off.

"Hi, Brad."

"Hi, Jess. Do you think we can . . . you know . . . talk? In private?"

Gracefully, Jessie slipped out of the swing. She looked at Skeff and politely, sweetly asked him to leave. It was practically music to Brad's ears.

"I guess you want to be alone when you tell Mr. Billboard you never want to see him again . . . right?"

Jessie didn't answer.

"Don't let the pretty boy sweet talk you!" said Skeff, looking at Brad. "I mean, who is he, anyway? Just some average ball player who used to be on a billboard."

Brad looked away. The words stung only because they were true.

"Goodbye, Skeff," said Jessie, and the look on Skeff's face made Brad feel almost sorry for him.

When they were alone, Brad sat down on the grass. Jessie sat beside him.

"Are you and Skeff . . ." he began. "I mean, is he your . . ."

Jessie shook her head. "He just keeps hanging around. I can't stand him."

"I'm sorry I was such a jerk."

She thought a moment before she replied. "It's all right."

"I'm not even sure how it happened," he admitted. "I guess it just went to my head—the attention, the money . . . Everybody hates me, huh?"

"Nobody hates you, Brad. They're just a little fed up right now, but they'll get over it." She smiled. "I kept trying to imagine how I would have felt if it had happened to me. I probably wouldn't have acted any better than you did."

"Ya' think?"

"And it was partly our fault, too—I mean, letting you get away with that high-and-mighty stuff. I don't think you would have acted differently if we hadn't started treating you differently. Let's face it, Brad, it was kind of a rush for all of us. We all got a kick out of saying, 'I know the billboard guy.'"

She was touching his arm, as she had that rainy day in his kitchen. He remembered how Miranda had body-slammed Gino, and decided he liked Jessie's approach much better.

"Do you think you're going to model anymore?" she asked.

"Hard to say." Brad leaned back on his elbows. "It's a lot more complicated than it looks."

"If I tell you something," said Jessie, "will you promise not to laugh?"

"I promise."

"That picture of you from the flyer—the one where you're doing chin-ups—I tore it out. It's taped to my mirror." She was checking his expression out of the corner of her eye. "Does that bother you?"

"*Bother* me? No. It doesn't bother me!" He tilted his head at her. "You *know* it doesn't bother me." And as long as they were being honest, there was something else he wanted her to be clear on. "I never really liked Cass," he confessed. "I didn't! I never even thought she was pretty."

Jessie gave him a look that made him laugh.

"Okay. So she's *pretty.* Really pretty." He looked down at the grass. "But she's not . . . well, she's not . . . you." When Brad looked up, he knew he'd never seen a more beautiful shade of pink than the color that was flooding Jessie's cheeks. They were quiet for a moment.

"I'm glad that billboard's gone," he said, and meant it.

"So am I. Know why?"

When Brad shook his head, Jessie took his hand and whispered, "Because . . . I like having you all to myself."

"Really?"

In answer, she gave his hand a squeeze.

And he gave her his father's smile. His smile.

Brad went straight to the laundry porch and found his spikes exactly where he'd left them the day of the thunderstorm. A wave of guilt crashed in his stomach. They were stiff and caked with dirt, with the laces dried into grungy knots and clumps of dusty brown earth stuck between the spikes. He picked them up, grabbed an old rag, and carried them downstairs to the basement.

He was surprised to find his mother seated comfortably in the old recliner. She had a bandana tied kerchief-style around her hair. Even from across the basement, she smelled of Pine Sol.

She seemed so engrossed in the scrapbook that at first

Brad thought she didn't notice him. His first instinct was to be outraged that she'd invaded his privacy, but under the circumstances he opted not to voice his feelings. Mom had the monopoly on outrage today.

"You went out . . ." she said, her head still bent over a yellowing page.

"Yeah," said Brad, leaning against the sawhorse. "How'd you know?"

"I dragged it out of Nana." Mom looked up and there was a softness in her eyes Brad didn't expect.

He gave a wary smile. "She said she'd cover for me."

"Hmm." Mom lifted one eyebrow. "Now *she's* grounded."

Brad laughed. "Are you mad?"

"Well, you're still grounded, if that's what you mean. But Nana told me where you went, so I figured, if you were ready to admit that you'd been horrible, you'd learned your lesson."

Brad let out his breath. "I'm sorry I got so out of control."

Mom nodded. "I think I may be at least partially to blame for that. I don't think I was paying enough attention, to be honest. The party, for example—I should have investigated it more closely before I agreed to let you go." Mom closed the scrapbook and leaned forward in the chair. "Do you know why I allowed it?"

Brad shook his head.

"Because I thought it would give you a good close look at the way things are out there in the grownup world, at the Zoes and the Mirandas and the Joanna Tandys." She paused. "What did you think of them?"

Brad examined his dirty baseball shoes and thought a long moment before he answered. "Well, one thing's for sure," he answered solemnly. "Being with them sure made miss me Bernie Klemp!"

Mom's laughter told him he'd given the right answer, and he laughed, too.

When she got up and headed for the stairs, Brad put down his shoes and followed her. He could clean them later . . . He *would* clean them later. Right now, he wanted to finish his apologizing. His aunt was next on the list.

They found Jill in the kitchen, drinking lemonade with Nana, and listening to Meggie ramble on about her modeling career.

Mom's face registered shock. "*Your* modeling career?"

"Yes!" Meggie took a dainty sip of lemonade. "I'm a model now. But don't worry. I'm not gonna let it go to my head like Brad did!"

Brad turned to Jill. "I owe you a can of volumizing mousse."

"Forget it," said Jill, tousling his hair. She threw Meggie a playful look. "That stuff should come with a warning label: Keep out of reach of models."

Meggie laughed. "Don't worry about me. Now that I'm a model, I plan to singlehandedly bring back the natural look."

Brad took a deep breath. "It's a weird word—model."

His sister cocked her head. "What's weird about it?"

Brad searched for a way to explain what he meant. "A model is something that's supposed to represent something bigger. It's like, the most perfect example . . ."

"Like a model citizen," said Meggie.

"Right," said Brad. "And fashion models are supposed to represent people—but what's weird is that they do everything they can to be as different as possible from regular people."

"Interesting." Mom gave him a little grin.

But Brad wasn't finished. "Everybody's always saying that looks don't really matter."

Jill laughed. "Try not to spread that philosophy around. It'll put me out of a job."

"Exactly!" said Brad. "Looks do matter. Maybe they shouldn't, but they do. I mean, c'mon . . . being great-looking can get you places in the world." He frowned. "Why won't anyone ever admit that?"

Nana shrugged. "Because it's superficial. Of course, I suppose pretending it's not true is even more superficial."

Brad leaned back in his chair. "You don't expect smart people to say they don't care about being smart. Same with great athletes. So why do beautiful people have to feel like they should apologize for being beautiful, or pretend they don't really care that they are?"

"Good question . . ." came a voice from the screen door. Everyone turned to see T.J. letting himself in.

"I'd like to know what T.J. thinks," said Meggie. "He's been eye candy a lot longer than Brad." She looked up at T.J.

T.J. thought a moment. "Everyone wants to be noticed. And being good-looking gets you noticed." He tugged Meggie's hair, but looked directly at Jill when he added, "Once you've got everyone's attention, you're halfway there."

Brad nodded. "Maybe that's it. Maybe being beautiful is like having a really long head start."

"That makes sense," said Mom. "No one wants to feel they *need* a head start. So they scoff at being . . . what's that term again, Meggie?"

". . . Eye candy."

"Eye candy. And hope their other talents and abilities shine through."

"It's just plain old good manners," said Nana, waving her hand. "If you're born with a gorgeous mug, you don't rub other people's noses in it."

"When you get right down to it, then," said Brad, "being good-looking is just a lucky coincidence."

"In T.J.'s case," said Meggie, waggling her eyebrows, "*very* lucky."

Brad laughed, then watched in surprise as T.J. walked directly to Jill and kissed her on the cheek.

Finally, thought Brad, grinning across the kitchen at T.J. *Score one for the boys!* And the way T.J. grinned back told Brad that his buddy was thinking the same thing.

Brad walked Jessie to school on the first day, and they paused at the ball field, laughing when they saw that the billboard now featured three old ladies wearing flannel nightgowns.

"If you ask me," teased Jess, "it's a major improvement."

Brad caught up to Trevor and Scott at lunch. To his surprise, they'd saved him a seat.

"You guys still talking to me?" he asked, a little choked up.

"Sure." Scott shrugged. "It's gonna take more than your swelled head to come between three years of Little League and a season of Junior Babe Ruth!"

It wasn't until after they'd traded their sandwiches that Brad noticed Trevor's shirt. It was the same striped one that Brad had modeled on the billboard, only Trevor's was white-and-blue, instead of green.

"Yankees colors!"

"You know it, man!"

It was the first high five of the school year.

Later, in history, Brad apologized to Bernie Klomp, but Bernie told him he really shouldn't be sorry at all.

"Why not?" said Brad. "It was crummy of me to say you were fat."

"It was crummy," said Bernie, "but it was true. I cut down on junk food, and you know what? I got all new jeans for school because the old ones were too big." He gave Brad a proud smile, and his good bone structure was more visible than ever. "I feel great, man. Thanks to you."

As it turned out, no one was holding a grudge toward

Brad at all. In science he noticed that Norman was wearing a very fashionable new sweater, and in gym he discovered that half the guys he knew had updated their haircuts, just in time for the new semester. As Jessie had predicted, they'd forgotten everything, and were treating Brad the way they always had.

All in all, it was the best first day of school he could remember. It was *after* school that things started to get a little sticky.

Skeff and his pals were waiting on the field.

"Hey, Wilson," said Skeff, pointing toward the billboard full of old ladies. "Is that you in the red flannel nightie?" He roared with laughter. "Or are you the one in the pink fuzzy slippers?"

Brad dragged his hand through his hair and kept walking.

"Where ya' going, Pretty Boy? Home to shave your legs?"

"Skeff, don'tcha think this is gettin' kinda old?"

"If ya' stay, I'll let you borrow my eyelash curler!"

"Listen, Parker . . ." said Brad, clenching his fists. He was tired of Skeff's insults, but what was worse, he was surely the only guy on the ball field who knew what an eyelash curler was.

And then it hit him. He *wasn't* the *only* one. He stopped walking.

"You think you're pretty tough, don'tcha, Skeff?" said Brad, his voice level. "Callin' me a Glamour Boy and all that. Well, I have a question for ya'. How come *you* know so much about eyelash curlers, huh? How come you know the name of every kind of makeup there is?" Brad whirled to face Norman. "Norm, what's mascara?"

Norman shrugged.

Brad turned to Bernie. "Do you know the difference between a manicure and a pedicure?"

Bernie shook his head.

"Don't worry," said Brad, "you can ask Parker. He knows all about it! I know he knows, because he's been ridin' me about this junk all summer." He turned back to Skeff. "Tell us, Skeff . . . or is it Skeff*ina*? How did you become such a cosmetics expert, anyway?"

"Sisters," Skeff muttered. "I have sisters . . . okay?"

But everyone was laughing too hard to hear him.

Brad turned and continued walking. "Don't start with the billboard business, either," he said over his shoulder. "Cause that's gettin' old, too."

The mention of the challenge seemed to bring Skeff back to life. "Well, then, why don't we get it over with?" Skeff shoved his hand into his glove and tossed Brad a bat. "You hit the billboard, right here, right now, and I swear I'll never rag on you again."

Brad picked up the bat. "Deal."

Word spread so quickly that kids were flocking from the school to the bleachers before Brad was even in the batter's box. He saw Jessie hurrying over from the girls' gym. Pamela Hartley was close on her heels.

Bernie Klemp slipped easily into his chest protector and stood behind the plate. "Go for it, Brad," he said.

Jessie had reached the backstop. She took a place behind it, anxiously hooking her fingers into the wire links. Out of the corner of his eye, Brad could see Pamela purposely squeezing in beside Jessie at just the right angle to obstruct her view completely.

"Pamela . . ." said Jessie sweetly.

"Yes?"

"Move it or *lose* it! And I mean *now.*"

The next thing Brad knew, Pamela was heading for the bleachers . . . fast. He laughed so hard he almost dropped the bat—which was why he was so stunned when the first pitch came screaming in and hit him square on the shoulder.

"Hey!" yelled Bernie. "Are you crazy? He wasn't even in the box!"

Skeff shrugged. "My mistake."

Skeff's fastball must have been improving, because Brad's arm *hurt.* The force of it had knocked him off balance, and he was on his knees in the dirt, holding his shoulder. Trevor and Scott rushed over to help—Brad wondered where Jessie was.

"Looks like no one's gonna hit the billboard today," crowed Skeff.

"That's what you think!"

Brad looked up to see Jessie snatching a bat from the bag behind the backstop. He wondered if it was just dumb luck that she'd grabbed a nice aluminum Easton—a short, light bat that happened to be perfect for someone her size.

Jessie stepped into the left-hander's box and swung the bat around over her left shoulder.

"What are you doing?" asked Brad, forgetting the throbbing in his shoulder.

"I'm a lefty," said Jessie.

Brad opened his mouth, then closed it. That wasn't what he'd meant.

Skeff was laughing from the mound. "So your little girlfriend's coming in to save the day for you?"

"You were the one who practically busted his shoulder," said Trev, helping Brad to the dugout.

Jessie thumped her bat hard on home plate. "Like you said, Skeff. Why don't we get it over with?" She brought the bat back into position.

Brad couldn't believe it. She had an excellent stance!

"So pitch already!" cried Bernie.

Skeff began his windup. Brad could tell from the look on his face that he wasn't going to hold anything back just because Jessie was a girl. He made a silent vow to murder Skeff if that ball so much as grazed her.

The pitch came blazing toward the batter. Brad could see Jessie's eyes pulling the ball into focus . . . waiting . . . watching . . . and then . . .

. . . *Pop!* And *what* a pop!

"That's outta here!" screamed Bernie.

"Yesssss!" cried Trev and Scott together.

Brad, on the other hand, kept his mouth clamped shut. He knew if he opened it he would have hollered *I love you, Jess!*

Not that anyone would have been paying attention. Because at that moment everyone was focused on the vicious fly ball that seemed about to collide with three old ladies in red nightgowns and pink slippers.

Brad was on his feet in the dugout. "It's going . . . !"

Skeff was on his face on the mound. "It's going . . ."

And then it was gone . . . *over* the billboard.

Brad's mouth dropped. *Over?*

Jessie was very calmly brushing the dust from her hands. "That counts, doesn't it?"

The answer was a shout of awed amazement from every kid on the ball field, Brad included.

"I thought so," said Jessie. Smiling, she stepped out of the box and made her way toward the dugout.

"How's your shoulder?" she asked Brad.

"What shoulder?"

"You're not mad, are you?" A flash of worry darkened her eyes. "I mean, that I did it, and you . . ."

Brad shook his head. The fact of the matter was that he had never been less mad about anything in his life.

Jessie was smiling, and Brad couldn't tell if the pounding he was hearing was the sound of Skeff's fist hitting the mound or the beating of his heart. "Jessie . . ."

She was lifting her chin toward him. "Yes?"

Brad reminded himself to close his eyes . . . After all, this was the kiss he was going to remember the rest of his life. He wanted it to be perfect.

And it was.